The Widow's Watch

The Widow's Watch

Shaw Manor
~ Book 3 ~

MARK E. WELCH

Cover design by Eva Gustafsson, All Design Studio
alldesignstudio.com

Back cover text by Trish Atwater Smith

Published in the U.S.A.

ISBN: 979-8-9986232-3-3
Library of Congress Control Number: 2022917280

Ghosts, Angels & Demons

Within the world of the living, it is hypothesized that a realm of the paranormal and supernatural exists in the shadows, and only the lucky few are offered a glimpse into it. Perhaps it might be a shadow that is perceived from the corner of one's eye that leaves a person uneasy. An unexplained noise occurs when there is only quietness. A nightmare or a dream that seems all too real or even a full apparition of a spirit. Such events are purported phenomena described in myth and lore and modern-day life, yet to be validated as scientific fact.

Fact or fiction these hypotheses are yet to be proved, and still, some of the living believe and place their faith in such. Perhaps they are correct in their assumptions. Or are they?

Whether true reality or a fabrication within one's mind, such happenstances seem to exist and can be terrifying.

~ M.E. Welch, Author

CONTENTS

CHAPTER 1
Aerin

The Penders' adoption of Vicky went seamlessly, and with the birth of their first son, Aerin, the following years were both peaceful and rewarding for Bill and Cathy. Their daughter Gaea and her adopted sister were elated with their new baby brother and lavished affection upon him whenever possible.

Piddles had bonded with the newborn as the breed was known to do. German people had bred the dog to be a home protector and she was living up to her legacy. The now extinct Bullenbeisser, the Great Dane, and possibly terrier made up the bloodline of Piddles' Boxer lineage. She had nearly abandoned the girls for the most part during the evenings to lie on the floor in Aerin's nursery, taking up the decades-long job of sentry, guarding the child while the manor's inhabitants slept.

Bill Pender was satisfied that his home had remained silent. Except for a few "bumps and thuds" that came from the attic, he was overjoyed by the renewed peace and calm. In the back of the author's mind, he did harbor a small resentment. His daughter Gaea, as well as his wife, possessed a gift that he did not have. They had the ability to sense and even see the two spirits that resided in Shaw Manor. Vicky had not shown she had the ability to be sensitive, although she claimed she did. Her previous incident in the attic had convinced her that she was a sensitive also. However, her sister Gaea had no such beliefs about her.

The paranormal aside, Bill had other concerns that worried him here in the now. Both Gaea and Vicky were seventeen years old and had moved on from dolls to boys. His responsibilities outside of the manor, which included attending book signings and other affairs related to his profession, had shifted to those of a concerned father. His success as a published author of over fifteen bestselling novels and five major motion pictures had awarded him the luxury of no longer having to do mandatory book signings. *The Emissary* was nominated for best picture of the year, and along with his other associated awards, his existence had been redefined. Thus, William Pender had made the decision to play dad for an upcoming and undetermined length of time, happily receding from the public eye. There were still a few events that he had committed to attending, the award ceremonies had been a major one. Bill had to admit that although it had been uncomfortable walking the red carpet, it had been a remarkable experience. Once it was over, though, he was quite happy to go back to being just Bill Pender, the writer.

He still had one scheduled event to attend before the end of the year. The exhibit for Captain Wilbur H. Shaw, his ship the Constance, and her crew was to be unveiled in Bath at the Maine Maritime Museum. One William Pender was to do the honor of cutting the ribbon, not that that was of much consequence to the author. He wanted to see the display and how the museum presented the lives of such sea-faring men. Along with the donation he had made to the museum on behalf of Captain Shaw, he also believed he owed the man as much since his own family occupied Shaw Manor.

Cathy could not have been happier with her life. Her business had taken off in a remarkable way. She now ran three antiquities shops. With the addition of her new partner Jeremy Winters and his two stores in New York City, they ran five shops together. The culmination of the business was keeping Doctor Catherine Pender remarkably busy.

After the death of the love of his life Jack Jefferson, Jeremy had spent a short stint at Pepper and Pepper before concluding that his passion resided in rugs and tapestries, not paperbacks and magazines. Publishing was not his cup of tea. Robert Pepper had understood, and with a bit of prodding from his wife Dorothy, he agreed to let the man resign and pursue his dream.

Aerin Pender had grown into a rambunctious young lad. At age seven, his curiosity and imagination knew no bounds. The boy feared nothing, and it took everything Bill had to keep the child in check. Numerous times he had to pluck his son from the back stone wall as he tried to climb up to peer at the ocean some fifty feet below. Bill nor Cathy believed in excessive forms of physical punishment for any of their children. However, a swift smack on the boy's rear end was needed from time to time, and it seemed to do the trick. If only for the indiscretion on that day. The following morning was a new adventure.

The start of school was Bill's reprieve from the raising of his son. Gaea and Vicky were angels compared to Aerin. As he had promised the girls, if both kept at least a B average, they would get cars. Secretly, Bill winced every time they ran into the manor with their report cards. He was terrified of having his two daughters driving at such an early age. Both had proven not only to be excellent scholars, maintaining a near straight A average, but their maturity also warranted the prize. How they both dealt with their peers and boyfriends, as well as their help around the manor, including dealing with Aerin, was nothing short of remarkable.

The housekeeping staff also helped greatly in dealing with the upbringing of his son. Bill had dismissed the every-other-week service that he had been using. With the two girls and the birth of Aerin, both he and his wife agreed on employing a staff. Fortunately, they did not have any trouble in the process. Their first hire was a housekeeper who would be in overall charge of the cleanliness and the fulfillment of the manor's needs, be it supplies or other necessities. In addition, two housemaids had been added to perform the daily cleaning of the manor. Up until the age of five, when Aerin started school, a nanny was employed to help with his care as well as to see to the girls' needs. As the years passed by, the nanny had finally been let go.

Bill had also hired a groundskeeper to maintain the manor's outdoor areas, including the cemetery. Maine winters took their toll on the buildings and the rest of the estate. It seemed prudent to have someone who could see to the task. He, in turn, was given the job of hiring people who would perform the major repairs that arose periodically around the manor, relieving Bill of this responsibility and giving him more time to focus on writing.

The housekeeper and the housemaids were live-in staff and took up residence within the far side of the manor in the newly built quarters that took up a third of the attic space. The renovation had been simple, first with framing, then running the electrical and plumbing for the additional bedrooms. Extending the servant stairwell had proven to be a slight problem as it interfered with a chimney that rose up through the roof for the furnace. The architect had simply designed them to wind around the existing brick. Once done, the result was simplistic but blended with the manor perfectly. Although small, the three bedrooms that were created were cozy, each with a window that either looked out over the ocean or the courtyard of the estate. One of the rooms had its own private bath. The others shared a common bathroom that had been designed to allow two people to use its facilities at the same time. Neither Cathy nor Bill wanted the manor staff to take up the guest rooms that might be needed for friends. The addition was the perfect solution.

The groundskeeper, however, lived over on the mainland and sustained a minimum of forty hours per week. He was on call as needed for emergencies and other happenstance. Bill did have an office building off from the side of the garage that had a bathroom as well as a cot in case the man had to stay for the night.

The Penders had foregone the addition of a house chef as both Bill and Cathy enjoyed cooking. With Vicky's visits to the Pepper Mansion in Bar Harbor, she had become a fine cook herself. The tutelage from Dorothy had been paying dividends to Bill's stomach. One evening she began to talk of attending a culinary school after graduating high school. Gaea had quite different plans. She had dreams of pursuing a degree in parapsychology because of what had happened to her and Jack Jefferson at the manor. The paranormal fascinated her.

Bill and Cathy had taken both girls along with their son to pick out cars. The day-long affair amounted to lunch at the Fat Kat BBQ & Restaurant in South Portland before heading to Jeff's Motors. The company had a massive assortment of new and used vehicles, including Ford, Chevy, Plymouth, and more. Bill wanted to purchase used vehicles for the girls' first cars, but Cathy had stood firm and demanded that they would have brand new ones. Her husband reluctantly conceded.

Upon first sight of the vast complex, Bill cringed, feeling they might have to get a hotel room or come back for a return visit. Neither was the case. The family was escorted around the two acres of cars in a large golf cart, which proved to be unnecessary as well. Once again, Bill had underestimated his daughters. The girls pulled out folded-up pages that had been torn from a magazine and unfolded them in unison.

"Jeep Wrangler," Gaea stated.

"Same," Vicky affirmed.

The salesperson drove off and moments later arrived at a section of the lot. Bill and Cathy looked on, seeing identical Jeep models, however in assorted colors. Gaea wanted midnight metallic black, and Vicky had chosen a subtle powder blue. Both girls took turns test-driving one of them, and after a quick private conversation, they both gave their approval of the vehicle. Neither of the colors was on the lot, so Bill had them special ordered.

The following month had proven to be annoying for Bill, with constant questions of "When is it coming?" and "Why is it taking so long?" from his daughters. If it were not for the staff and school, he would have put a trap door at the top of the spiral staircase that emptied onto the widow's watch, protecting the author within his dreamer's hideaway. The women who supervised the manor's day-to-day operations were experts at diversions, however, and knew when to apply them.

For the most part, Cathy had not been at home for any length of time. Her business seemed to be consuming her more than her husband would have liked. Twice in three months, she had flown to New York to help with Jeremy's store during his expansion beyond tapestries and rugs. He had no formal training; however, he did have a unique business sense. Jeremy also had a knack when it came to recognizing items that were not junk and had value, especially when it came to antiquities. Cathy had taken it upon herself to become a mentor for Jeremy and it was using up a great deal of her time. Bill had been managing things rather smoothly around the manor, the staff alleviating much of the burden allowing him time in dreamer's hideaway to write. He was having a wife withdrawal. Cathy worked long hours and when she did come home, she usually spent a little time with the family before heading off to bed. And off to bed to sleep was not what Bill had in mind. His wife was becoming a serious workaholic, and it was infringing on their love life.

Off the coast of York, Maine, a lobster boat was pulling its pots when one of the ropes snagged on something heavy. The winch screamed as it struggled to pull the wooden trap up from the bottom of the Gulf of Maine. Worried it would burn out, the deckhand began to haul the line by hand, helping the struggling motor. A few moments later, the captain joined to help and a black object that was wrapped in the line appeared at the surface of the water. "What the hell is that?" The deckhand asked.

"Let's get it on deck and unbind it. We need to save the pot." The captain instructed.

"Ayuh." The deckhand responded, struggling to drag the object aboard.

Cathy had taken the entire weekend off for a change. It was a delivery day of the girls' Jeeps, and Bill wanted the occasion to be special. The entire family stood out in front of Shaw Manor, as well as the staff, as the car transport truck arrived. Both Jeeps gleamed in the sun as they were driven one by one down to the drive and parked side by side. The girls were ecstatic, jumping around and hugging one another.

"What is that?" Cathy asked her husband. A third vehicle was being driven off from the truck. A new black Ford F-150 joined the two Jeeps.

"My new truck," Bill responded. "I was driving the old one, and my foot went through the floorboard. I thought it was time."

"It is about time. That old truck of yours is what? Over twenty years old?"

He looked at his wife and smiled weakly. "I'm nostalgic."

"Nostalgic my ass. More like a junk collector." She scolded. "Please tell me you are not keeping the old one."

"Well, I thought maybe I could have it restored."

"What!" Cathy exclaimed, slapping his arm.

"Just kidding, baby. Easy. They are going to haul it away. I got a hundred bucks on the trade-in."

"You could have got more if you had junked it like you did with my old car."

"You are an evil woman." He said, grinning.

Gaea chose to take her first drive up to Ogunquit Beach, where her friends liked to hang out. Vicky followed her sister in her own Jeep. Bill and Cathy climbed into Bill's new truck, which was loaded with every feature imaginable. One, that Cathy loved: Bench seats!" She exclaimed, sliding over to sit next to her husband.

"I know how you hated the buckets in the old one. But it's convertible. The middle pulls up for storage."

"I love it. Where are we going?"

"I was thinking maybe an afternoon trip to the White Mountains. You know, like we did with your first Land Rover."

"That seems like an eternity ago."

"Our last one was before Gaea was born." Bill reminded her.

"Mount Washington Hotel for lunch?" She asked.

"Maybe. Or perhaps we could just stop at a random café or restaurant along the way. It doesn't matter to me. I have my wife for a couple of days for a change."

Cathy frowned. "I'm sorry, this entire new venture for me is getting out of hand, isn't it?"

"You know I support you one hundred percent, " he said, turning the key and starting the engine. "I just get lonely. I miss you, babe."

"I miss you too. Look, I promise things are going to calm down. Jeremy can run his business confidently. And I am promoting Denise to General Manager of my shops."

"That young girl?" Bill asked.

"Bill, she has a master's degree in Archeology. She is far from a child."

"Time flies, doesn't it?" Bill said, drifting momentarily off.

"It does. Now get out, I am driving."

The lobster boat had tied up at the last available berth in a bustling York Harbor to unload. The season was booming, and boats were returning with record numbers. "It looks like a Doberman Pincer, doesn't it Skip?" The deckhand asked.

"Damn ugly if you ask me."

"What are you going to do with it?"

The captain scratched his chin in thought. "It might be worth something. Need to find out just what it is. We'll load it in my truck, and I will stop at that museum up in Wells. They might have an idea if it's junk or somethin' else."

The deckhand squatted down and braced to lift the statue. Surprisingly, it had little weight and he placed it into the captain's pickup easily. "What the heck?"

"It was probably full of water and drained out."

"That thing nearly burned out our winch."

"We were also hauling a full trap."

"That's true, Skip. I guess that is why you are the captain."

"Day off tomorrow. We'll let the pots soak, and I'm going to have the winch checked out. We don't need it goin' down halfway through a string."

"You got it, Skip."

As the first mate sped off in his own truck, the captain looked at his find. "Damn ugly it is." He muttered.

CHAPTER 2
Scion of the Seas

Robert Pepper hung up from his weekly video conference. As usual, it was rather mundane. He was beginning to wonder if he needed to keep attending them at all. The publishing house that he owned was going along nicely, even with him living on Mt. Dessert Island, Maine. His semi-retirement had worked out famously, and his impulsive wedding and the purchase of the mansion in Bar Harbor had reaped dividends for his health as well as his love life. Marrying his long-time secretary was the best decision that he had ever made. A light tap on his office door drew his attention.

"Bobby?" His wife asked quietly, opening the door. "Are you finished?"

"Yes, Dottie. Come in."

Bob's wife had recently turned seventy, yet her beauty astounded him every time he looked at her. He reflected on the time that he had hired her. A strong-willed woman of twenty-five who, although respectful, was not afraid to put her boss in his place when needed. Her looking out for him had begun from the first day she started as personal secretary to the head of Pepper and Pepper Publishing by organizing not only his professional schedule but also his personal life. Within a noticeably brief period, Bob could see a vast improvement in his efficiency. As the years passed, things became more personal as she became involved in his health. Making his doctor's appointments, arranging for, and even making some of his lunch meals herself, taking exceptional care to make sure they were healthy. There was no need for him to know that the mayo she was using was low-fat. Her switching him to whole wheat bread took some getting used to, but Bob grew to like it better than white.

Dottie walked to her husband and wrapped her arms around him. He was tall, but he had lost nearly two hundred pounds. Robert Pepper was a fit and healthy seventy-three-year-old.

"You know," Bob began, "we have never taken a proper honeymoon."

"The last seven years have been a honeymoon for me." She answered.

He leaned down and kissed her. "You are too good to me."

"Vicky Pender wants to come up this weekend."

"Fine with me. I can let our driver know to go pick her up."

Dottie smiled. "No need. It seems that both she and Gaea have brand-new Jeeps. Bill had promised that if they maintained a certain grade point average, he would buy them both cars. He made good on that promise, so she is going to drive herself up."

Bob shook his head. "It seems like yesterday that those two girls were playing with dolls, and Vicky...I remember her here making cookies with you in the kitchen."

"She is planning on going to culinary school," Dottie remarked. "She loves to cook and would like to open a restaurant."

"She certainly has the gift," Bob said, breaking the embrace with his wife. "What are we doing today?"

"Laundry." She said matter of factly.

"Honey, we have a staff for that!"

"Not our clothing and not my bedsheets that we sleep in. Now scoot!" Dottie scolded, shooing him towards the door.

"I've been promoted!" Denise Bastien exclaimed, throwing her arms around her husband's neck.

"Oui?" Jean-Claude Bastien, curator of the Wells Museum, asked. He had held the position for over eight years since Catherine Pender's departure to pursue her own ventures. His romance with his wife began shortly after taking the position as he began to collaborate with her from time to time. Dr. Pender would send Denise to the museum with artifacts she needed to identify or to have her own hypotheses confirmed. Bastien had been taken with the girl the moment he laid eyes on her, and her passion for antiquities and archeology further flamed his interest. After she had completed her four-year degree at the University of Maine at Orono, he asked for her hand in marriage. The summers in between her academic years away had been nothing less than perfection, although he missed her terribly when she was away. His work and her studies passed the time until school breaks when she could return.

Their four-year engagement started as Denise began the quest for her master's degree. Her choice to study at the University of New England in Biddeford changed Bastien's life. She moved into his house on Biddeford Pool, a ten-minute drive to the campus of UNE. The house was more of a two-bedroom cottage with one bath, but it sat directly on a beautiful stretch of private beach with a view of rocky coastline, and the sight and sound of the ocean crashing on the rocks was loved by the couple. Jean-Claude inherited the house shortly after taking the position at the Wells Museum. The sudden death of his aunt and his being the only beneficiary proved to be a blessing, however bittersweet. At the time, he had no thoughts of becoming romantically involved and getting married, but his introduction to Denise was a game changer.

The couple had been married less than a year. Denise had chosen to work full-time for Dr. Pender and wait before starting her own Doctorate, another choice that proved to be a good decision for both. "Jean, Cathy has promoted me to her General Manager as well as chief curator for her shops!"

"That is wonderful! You deserve it. You have worked so hard, baby."

"And look at this." She said, handing her husband an envelope.

Jean-Claude looked at his wife questioningly as he opened it. His eyes went wide as he looked at the check. "Denise, this is a check for fifty thousand dollars. I do not get it."

"She gave me a signing bonus and said it also contained bonus pay for my loyalty over the years."

He read it again before focusing on the notation portion of the check which read: "Happy Honeymoon."

"Honey, it says…"

"I know, I know!" She said happily, dancing around in a circle. "But we don't have to use it for that. We must talk about it, OK?"

"Yes, of course! But can we at least go out for dinner?"

"Absolutely!" Denise exclaimed, jumping back into his arms and kissing him passionately.

Captain Patricia Hilton stood at the helm of the research vessel Scion of the Seas. The refitted two hundred- and fifty-five-foot ship had just undergone a complete overhaul at Bath Shipyard in Maine. Built in 1968, the former icebreaker had been converted into the most advanced scientific vessel afloat. The forty-year-old woman was formidable, standing at over six feet tall. Her long jet-black hair did not hint at her Norwegian lineage however, her piercing blue eyes did. As the two tugs released the ship, she called out a heading and speed. The Scion cut through the Atlantic, heading northeast. "Contact the Archaean Horizon. We should be joining her in a few hours." Hilton commanded.

"Aye, Captain." a crew member answered.

Captain Hilton had relinquished her captaincy of the Archaean to her first Janice DeWight when T & B Maritime Archeological Expeditions purchased the Scion of the Seas. The success of the work that doctors Jeffrey Tarpon and Roland Brambilla had achieved was nothing short of remarkable and various societies, as well as universities, had taken notice. Grants followed, and with the personal wealth of the two scientists, they were able to procure the new vessel. Donations of equipment from other resources, including the governments of Italy and Canada, had made the ship a leading force in maritime research. Alongside the Archaean Horizon, the two ships would be formidable in their field of expertise.

The Archaean Horizon was now sitting one hundred and eighty nautical miles off the coast of Nova Scotia, floating over a WWII German U-Boat yet to be fully identified. Its submersible Aquabot had made a few passes over the wreck, however the boat's markings had yet to be uncovered. At seven hundred seventy-five meters, conditions were challenging. The advanced systems on the Scion of the Seas would help greatly with the new discovery. Captain DeWight reached for a telephone that hung on the bulkhead of the bridge. She punched in a three-digit number and waited.

"Brambilla." A voice answered.

"Doctor, the Scion of the Seas is underway and should be here in a few hours."

"Excellent. I am anxious to see Jeffery again."

"As I am to see Patricia." She replied.

"Keep me informed, please."

"Yes sir, you bet." She hung up the phone.

At thirty-nine years old, Janice DeWight looked nothing like Patricia. Standing at a mere five foot six inches tall, she did not appear formidable. On the contrary, as the crew had come to find out, she was a firecracker. She kept her red hair cropped short, and her blue eyes were sharp and keen. DeWight was a stickler for protocols due to her prior service in the US Navy. Being similar to her counterpart Captain Hilton, Captain DeWight had zero tolerance for safety violations and spent a great deal of time walking through and inspecting the Archaean Horizon. She had written up a crewmember more than once for not conforming to safety protocols. At sea, one lapse in judgment could cost a life. Not on her watch. Not under her command.

Her passion for the sea was equaled only by her feelings for Patricia. The two had grown up together and were separated only by career choice upon graduating from high school. Both went to sea; however, Patricia chose the merchant marines and rose quickly through the ranks. She was captaining her first tug by the time she was twenty-five. In contrast, Janice chose college and NROTC to become a line officer serving on a submarine tender in the US Navy. Choosing to resign her commission four years later, she re-joined Captain Hilton as executive officer on the Archaean Horizon. After seven years together, they were separated once again. This time, by captaincy, that seemed to be, at this point, a blessing. For the near future, it seemed that the Archaean Horizon and the Scion of the Seas would be sailing together.

Captain DeWight walked across the bridge and stood over the shoulder of a young girl who was tending to a computer station. "How are we doing?" The captain asked.

"Holding steady, Ma'am." She answered.

"Thank Neptune for dynamic positioning."

The dynamic positioning system had been added on the Horizon's last refit and was essential for holding the ship in position when in deep water as she was now. The computer-driven system used the ship's propellers as well as its thruster to keep the ship from drifting away from its target that lay on the seabed. If the seas were reasonably calm, the system worked perfectly. The system was shut down in case of a storm, and the Archaean Horizon dealt with the situation as needed. Once the seas calmed, the ship would return, and the system would be reactivated, resuming the task at hand. The operator of the system had to monitor and make simple corrections to compensate for drift due to the wind and sea conditions.

"Good work, Darlene." The captain said. "I am going to the galley to grab a coffee. Want something?"

"I'm good, thank you anyway. I'm being relieved soon."

"Of course." She replied, turned, and left the bridge.

Billy Smyth was atop the last pole before the power line fed onto the Shaw Estate and then to the manor. Southern Maine Power routinely performed maintenance on lines that cut through wooded areas. Smyth had been tasked with keeping power lines free from tree growth, a job that took place once a year and usually in the fall. Today he and Doug had been assigned to the Cape Neddick area. His partner had returned to the truck to retrieve their backup chainsaw, leaving Billy alone. As he hung from the pole in boredom waiting, he happened to glance down, and that is when he noticed her. Walking through the trees was a blonde woman in a long blue dress. From forty feet up, he could not see her face and found it odd that a woman should be out for a walk in a dress such as that.

"Hello?" He called down. The woman did not respond but disappeared into the dense foliage silently instead.

"I'm here, Billy," Doug called, appearing at the base of the pole. "What's up?"

"Did you see that?"

"See what?"

"The woman walking through the woods."

Doug looked around and shook his head. "Nothing around here but the chipmunks and squirrels. I don't see a woman."

"Forget it," Billy said and returned to work.

CHAPTER 3
The Housekeepers' Quarters

Aerin Pender tried the locked attic door as he had done numerous times. It remained steadfast and impervious to any attempt by the young boy to gain entry. On one occasion he had gone up to the widow's watch and was caught by his father and severely punished. No dessert for a month had been enough to curb his appetite to try a second time. Aerin had explored the rest of the manor several times, excluding the basement as it was locked up as tight as the attic.

There was another area of the manor that Aerin had not been able to get into. A staircase led down to the kitchen at the end of the second-story hall. Opposite the stairs was a door that was normally kept locked. Except for today. As he approached, he saw that it stood slightly ajar. Looking back over his shoulder and then down the stairs, he listened. He could hear women talking in the kitchen, but it was silent up the stairs. He reached up and grasped the doorknob, pulling the door open. Peering up, he could see the steep staircase rise and turn sharply to the left. A hand railing ran along the stairwell before ending against a wall, and another railing on the opposite side had been placed to protect from someone falling into the void.

Aerin crept his way up, stopping just short of the landing. Peeking through the banisters, he saw a small area containing a lamp and a couple of chairs. There was a closed door to the left. He could also make out the beginning of a hallway that was not dissimilar to the one his bedroom was on. The hall was well-lit by overhead lights, but a wall blocked his view any further.

He stepped up onto the landing and walked the few feet necessary to be able to look down the hallway. About a third of the length of the third-story hall, he could see two more doors on the left as well as two on the right. All were open. At the far end was a door that was closed. The walls were covered in light green pastel wallpaper. The woodwork was natural oak that resembled that of the rest of the manor. A long rug runner stretched from the landing down to the end of the hall.

Aerin opened the first door and found a bedroom neatly made and half the size of his. The rest of the doors proved to be nearly the same. Bedrooms are all meticulously kept except for a linen closet. He approached the closed door at the end of the hall and reached for the doorknob.

After dismissing his staff for the evening, Dr. Jean-Claude Bastien sat on a metal folding chair, staring at the relic that rested on an examination table before him. The object had been dropped off by a local lobsterman, and after confirming that it was nothing more than a fake, the man said to keep it and left the museum. What Bastien did not tell the man was what he suspected of the statue's true origin. Standing, he walked to his office and opened the top drawer of a metal filing cabinet. Retrieving a bottle of whiskey as well as a lowball glass, he sat at his desk and ran his hand through his hair. He opened the bottle and shakily poured some of the amber liquid into the glass. Swallowing it, he looked at the telephone on his desk.

"I haven't been here in years!" Cathy said, sitting down at a bright pink table adorned with a blue mushroom-shaped umbrella with orange spots.

Bill placed the tray on the table and sat down across from his wife as she reached for a wrapped sandwich. "I have never been here," Bill said, handing her a paper plate. He divided the fries and handed her a napkin. "Nothing like ketchup in a foil baggie." He smiled and tore the corner off the packet with his teeth.

"You know, the girls are going to be pissed when they find out we stopped at Story Land," Cathy stated.

"They chose to go play with their new Jeeps. We can go to play with my new truck. Besides, I did not plan to stop here. It was purely the spur of the moment. And," Bill said softly, leaning towards his wife, "they don't have to know."

"Really? Then how are you going to explain this, Mr. Covert Operator?" Cathy asked, holding up the three-foot-tall stuffed rabbit Bill had won at a booth near Alice's Teacups ride. It was clearly tagged with the amusement park's logo.

"We will hide it."

"Not on your life! This is the first thing you have ever won for me! It is going in our bedroom."

"I could have bought it cheaper," Bill mumbled. "A hundred and fifty bucks." Cathy threw a French fry at him and took a sip of her cola. "Is there anything we haven't seen here?" He asked.

"It is a shame that the water ride is closed for repairs. I would have liked to have gone on that one." Cathy admitted.

"What? And ruin the giant rat?" Bill replied, grinning.

"It's a rabbit, you jerk." She said, hugging the stuffed animal.

Bill started loading up the plastic tray with their trash. He slurped down the last of his iced tea and put it with the rest. "Done with yours?" He asked.

"Yup." She answered and handed it to him. He turned and walked across the bright yellow cobblestones toward a trash bin.

Cathy leaned back and closed her eyes, taking in the sounds and smells of the park. It had been years since she had been to Story Land. Her father had taken her when she was young, along with a boy that she thought might have been her cousin, although she could not remember his name. She recalled her dad telling her that they were having a family visit from Canada and that she would meet her Aunt Clara, but it had been so long ago that the memory had faded. Jeff or something like that might have been the kid's name. She had thought that he was weird.

She laughed at the thought. Cathy did remember that the day had been magical and why would it not have been? A six-year-old girl in a magical land filled with endless things to explore and experience. She regretted not bringing Gaea to Story Land. There were plenty of trips to Fun Town, Old Orchard Beach, and other places. Somehow, Story Land had never crossed her mind. Leave it to Bill to rediscover a place that was so special to her as a child.

She opened her eyes. Bill was standing in the center of the courtyard, still holding the tray and looking around at the small buildings that made up the area. He had a broad smile on his face, and it made her happy. What better place to take a writer of fiction than a magical land that was built on the same? Magical things brought on magical thoughts and dreams. Some individuals could weave those experiences into their own and create an alternative reality that people could enjoy. Some did it through visualization and physical experience, as Walt Disney had mastered. Some did it through music. Cathy's husband created magic through his writing and words, and people became lost within it. She closed her eyes again, losing herself in her own magical place.

It was not late; in fact, it was barely three in the afternoon yet. Bastien could not get Dr. Catherine Pender on the phone, and it was infuriating. "So, it was a Friday? Big deal." He mused. He knew that Dr. Pender never took time off. She had the work ethic and hours of an emergency room doctor doing an internship. So why wasn't she answering? He slammed down the phone and thought for a moment before grabbing his cell phone and scrolling through his contacts. Landing within the p's, he placed a call. "C'mon Bill, answer."

His phone rang in his ear several times before transferring to an automated message informing the caller that the answering was full. "Dammit!" Bastien grabbed his coat and ran out of his office. He paused and locked the lab door sealing the artifact inside. Reaching onto a nearby shelf, he picked up a magnetic sign that read "Danger No Entry" and placed it on the door. He locked the museum and ran to his car.

Aerin opened the door and found himself in a rather large bathroom. A countertop that supported two sinks was flanked by two toilet stalls and two more shower areas. Towels were stacked neatly upon shelves, and various toiletries adorned the room. A small table stood in the corner holding a vase of flowers. Something caught his eye, and he pushed the chair next to the table aside and dropped to his knees. Underneath the sink, he could see what looked like a small door in the wall.

In order to access the plumbing for the bathroom, the contractors had installed an access panel that led behind the wall. It was nicely framed and had two simple handles attached to it so that it could be easily opened. Large enough for a man to crawl through, it was huge for a seven-year-old boy. Crawling forward, Aerin grasped the handles in his hands and pulled. The hatch gave way easily, and he set it aside. Looking in, he saw mostly darkness. A dim light came in through a small window at the far end of the space.

He dug into his pocket, searching. He pulled out a bubble gum wrapper and a marble. He reached into his other pocket, and an open safety pin stuck his finger. "Ouch!" he whispered. Undaunted, he searched again and found what he wanted: his prized spy ring.

It had taken him almost six dozen boxes of cereal, one week at a time, before he could finally claim the top prize as advertised on the box. Most of them contained junk toys, but then, one morning, he was awarded the holy grail. Captain Trident's Spy Ring. It had a compass and secret compartment that Aerin had no clue what it was for. But, most importantly, the ring had a top-secret flashlight that was guaranteed for spies to find confidential documents in the darkest of places. He placed it on his finger and twisted the top of the ring. A light sprang from it. Not the brightest of lights, but enough to see a few feet in front of him.

Crawling waste deep into the void, Aerin looked around. The floor was wooden and very dusty. "The attic, " he whispered. Yes!" Several boxes lay strewn about. He could see through the dim light his ring provided what appeared to be the top of a staircase and a light bulb that hung unlit and motionless from a black wire.

Suddenly, he heard a voice behind him coming from the bathroom. He looked back to see a pair of hands grab him by his ankles. As the head housekeeper pulled him from the attic, he looked forward, the light from his ring momentarily shining upon the apparition of a young man with red hair. "Aerin, " it whispered, and a growl came from behind it that sounded like a girl.

Bill grabbed the rabbit from Cathy's hands, startling her, and ran off across the cobblestones, laughing. "Thief!" She cried, laughing, and charged after her husband. Bill was stopped short by a large man wearing a uniform.

"Sir, we do not condone stealing here at Story Land. I'm afraid you will have to come with me." Bill was out of breath and could barely talk as Cathy caught up.

"That is correct, officer. Rabbit thief he is. Lock him up."

"Honey!"

"You saw it! Drag him away!"

The officer was clearly amused and started to laugh. "This is not my first time seeing these types of shenanigans. But there are children about. Lots of them, so no running allowed."

A young boy was standing nearby listening and stuffing his face with cotton candy. "Yeah. No running."

"Come along, Cortland. This is none of our business, " a woman said, taking the boy by the hand and leading him away.

The officer returned the stuffed animal to Cathy, taking it from Bill. "Yours, I believe?"

It was nearly dark when Bill pulled the Ford into the garage. As he and Cathy got out of the cab, Bill noticed that his wife's Range Rover and his daughter's Jeep were parked neatly next to each other. Walking with his wife towards the door at the end of the garage, he ran his hand over the hoods of the vehicles. Both were cold. The girls had been home for some time.

As the couple entered the manor, their laughter was cut short. Before them, with her arms crossed, was the head housekeeper, Sarah Douglas. Sitting on a chair near her was Aerin. The Scottish woman had little patience for foolishness, and to Bill and Cathy, it seemed something was afoot. By the look on their son's face, he was the culprit. "Oh boy," Bill said softly.

CHAPTER 4
Questions, Problems, and Promises

The Archaean Horizon and the Scion of the Seas floated approximately seventy-five yards from one another. Identical platforms had been placed in the water amidship with a gangway that led up to their respective decks. A small boat was used to ferry the crew between the two research ships. As Jeffery Tarpon was running the new lab on the Scion of the Seas, Roland Brambilla was doing the same on the Horizon. It was necessary for the two scientists, as well as their staff, to be able to travel back and forth between the vessels.

With the excavation and research slated to begin early the next morning, the two captains and scientists were enjoying a seafood dinner in the Scion's captain's quarters. Both ships had executive-level chefs who oversaw meals for the crew and officers. They also performed as the captain's personal chef when the need arose. Such was this occasion as the new ship had arrived onsite. Dr. Tarpon stood holding up his glass of Pinot Grigio. "Here is to the Scion of the Seas, our newest addition to the fleet!" He exclaimed. The four clinked glasses and drank.

"I hardly think that two ships make a fleet, Jeffery." Dr. Brambilla said, setting his glass back on the table.

Tarpon waved his friend's comment off. "May we also toast our new captain of the Archaean Horizon, Janice DeWight!"

"Here, here!" Patricia Hilton shouted, and the four toasted and drank again.

"How is the dynamic positioning system working on the Scion?" Tarpon asked Captain Hilton.

"Just fine. Except for minor corrections, we have little or no drift."

"Same on the Horizon," DeWight added. "As long as the weather holds, we should be right as rain. At least for the next week or so."

"I agree, Janice," Patricia said. "I see no problems with resuming normal operations in the morning. I have my crew preparing the Scion as we speak. We will be ready."

"I would expect no less," Tarpon said. "You are both credits to your profession."

A young man arrived and placed steaming plates of Maine lobster in front of the foursome. That was followed by chilled Alaskan Dungeness crab legs and Atlantic mussels that appeared to be steamed in white wine and herbs. Fresh broccoli spears, mashed potatoes, fresh whole wheat rolls, tubs of melted drawn butter, and a side Caesar salad made up the meal. Brambilla nodded at the lad and smiled. "Please give the chef my compliments for yet another fine meal." He said, tucking a napkin under his chin.

"From all of us." Tarpon echoed. The young man nodded and left.

"I think the first order of business in the morning is to get Portunus in the water and down to our U-Boat. I hope it will perform as our friends over at MIT designed it to do."

"The robot is supposed to be the best that there is. Their robotics team arrived this morning to oversee its first dive. Supposedly, the new additions of high-resolution cameras, sensors, propulsion improvements, as well as many other additions, make our Aquabot obsolete." Brambilla stated.

"Maybe we can convince them to procure us a second one?" Janice asked, stuffing a piece of lobster in her mouth.

"I was hoping to have Dr. Laurent, the MIT team leader, join us. Unfortunately, she declined, citing too much to get done before tomorrow." Tarpon said.

"Any guesses on which boat our target is?" Hilton asked, attacking her salad.

"I do not make guesses," Brambilla stated. "However, the historical data suggests that it might be a U-116 that went missing on the 6th of October 1942 a few hundred miles east of here. We have no conclusive evidence, mind you."

"No evidence yet," Tarpon said, refilling his wine glass. He motioned to pass the bottle on but was waved off. "I, for one, am hoping to have that evidence tomorrow with the help of Portunus. If, and I emphasize *if* it is the U-116, this will be a momentous discovery."

"We shall see what the morning brings," Brambilla said.

Dr. Jean-Claude Bastien sat in his Volvo and beat the steering wheel with clenched fists. He had driven to Shaw Manor in the hope of finding the Penders. The staff had informed him that no one was home and that they were not expected to return until much later that evening. Infuriating as it was, he had no choice but to head for his own home and wait.

Gaea and Vicky had heard the scolding that their brother had received from Mrs. Douglas, and they wanted nothing to do with whatever was going on. They knew all too well not to cross that woman and avoided her like the plague. When they had to deal with the Scottish version of Nurse Ratchet, they were always polite and did what they were told. The wrath of her tongue was nothing either of them wanted to endure. When Aerin got into trouble, both girls looked at one another and shook their heads. The brat had made his bed and let him lay in it. Gaea and Vicky put on their headphones and returned to listening to music.

"You will sit in that chair, young man, until your parents arrive." Mrs. Douglas said sharply. "Of all the gumption! I have never seen such a thing! And don't you dare move!" Aerin had no intention of moving. And the threats he heard coming from the woman as she worked in the kitchen reinforced his fear. "If he were my child, he'd be in the woodshed getting the switch!" He heard her say.

Aerin was scared to the core of what he had seen in the attic and the additional terror which was being inflicted upon him from the head housekeeper was not helping him. He was sure of what he saw. It was a young man and he had spoken to Aerin just as he was yanked from the void. Terrifying as it was, he was curious. Why would there be a guy living in his attic? Who was he, and why was he there? And who had growled at him? Questions were overcoming his fear. Until his parents walked in the front door.

Cathy dropped her stuffed animal onto the floor of the great room and took in what was before her. Mrs. Douglas was standing to the side of her son, her arms crossed and her foot tapping on the floor. That was precisely when Bill sighed, "Oh, Boy." He turned on his heel to exit. "I think I left something in the truck, " he said and started to leave.

"Not a chance," Cathy said sternly. "He is your son as well. Keep your ass right here."

"But doesn't this qualify as a motherly duty?" He pleaded. The look he got from his wife turned the blood in his veins to ice.

Once Cathy had agreed to household staff, she demanded that it would be her to interview and hire the people that would see to the manor. Bill had readily agreed, thinking he did not want the chore anyway. What did he know about hiring people? Basically, he had one employee to deal with and always had. Himself. He had not anticipated his wife hiring the Scottish bitch from hell. The woman scolded everyone in the house who dared to step out of line. Never did Bill think that his sanctuary, his dreamer's hideaway, would become a real sanctuary.

Aerin fidgeted in the chair as his parents spoke with Mrs. Douglas. He strained to hear what they were saying, but they kept their voices low. Except for a few gestures Aerin could gather nothing from them. Until the three of them turned and glared at him.

Bastien arrived home. Nothing was going his way. He had used his phone to the point that it was dead, and he could not find his car charger. As he pulled up to the house, it was dark except for the motion sensor spotlight that flicked on as he pulled into the driveway. He stepped out of the car, grabbed his coat, and reached for his briefcase, which was not there. "Dammit. Jean, you idiot." He had left the satchel on his desk, and he remembered the car charger was inside of it. Rubbing his forehead, he fumbled with his keys and unlocked the front door.

"Honey?" He called out as he walked into the kitchen and turned on the light. He tossed his coat onto a chair and picked up a note left by his wife.

Baby,

I tried to call you. I had to run up to Bangor to pick up.

something for the shop. I will be home later tonight.

Love you!

Bastien sighed. How much bad luck could one man have in a single day? He needed a drink. Walking to the refrigerator, he opened it. Peering in, he saw right away that he was out of beer. "Dammit." He mumbled, shutting the door and walking out of the kitchen.

Aerin knocked lightly on his sister's bedroom door. With no immediate response he rapped on it harder. "What do you want, twerp?" Gaea called out.

He could hear the girls laughing. "Can I please come in? I need to talk to you. Mom and Dad don't believe me." Vicky opened the door to a pitiful-looking boy.

"I'm supposed to be in my room, but please?" Aerin was dressed in his Spiderman PJs. Vicky rolled her eyes, sighed, and let him in.

"Gaea!" He exclaimed and jumped up and into his sister's arms.

"What did you do now?" She asked cuddling her brother. Vicky climbed onto the bed and joined them.

"I was wrong, and I know that." He spoke. "But they won't believe me."

"Wrong about what?" Vicky asked.

"I went up to the third floor."

"What!?" Gaea exclaimed. "That is off limits, Aerin."

"I know, but I found a door in the maid's quarters."

"You are so screwed, Aerin," Vicky added.

He had tears in his eyes, and Gaea looked at him. "C'mon, do not be a baby. Tell us what happened. OK?"

"OK." He snuffled.

Cathy plugged her phone in and placed it on the nightstand. "Lots of missed calls from Jean-Claude but no voicemail." She spoke. "I hope there is nothing wrong. Maybe I should call him."

"At this hour? Call him in the morning." Bill yawned. "It's been a long day."

"But a good one." Cathy turned off the light and snuggled up next to her husband. "And I am off for two more days, mister."

"Why would he go up there?" Bill asked. "He knows better."

"He is a kid, Bill. Children are curious."

"I thought that Mrs. Douglas was going to kill the boy."

Cathy laughed and touched her husband's lips. "The woman is stern, but only with her words."

"I'm glad you think so. I've seen kinder women in a horror movie."

"Let me deal with our head housekeeper. In the meantime," Cathy was interrupted by a knock on the door. "Yes?"

"Mom?" Gaea asked. "Can we come in?"

Bill looked at his wife, shrugged, and chose to answer for her. "Yes, baby, you can come in." The bedroom door opened, and three children stood in the doorway. Cathy turned the light back on.

Bastian was beside himself with worry. At nearly midnight, his wife was still not home. He cursed himself for not having a proper landline installed and could not charge his cell phone. Public telephones were a thing of the past and he refused to bother his neighbors at such an hour. He knew that Denise was self-sufficient and could take care of herself. Yet, after the day's happenings, he was a nervous wreck. At a quarter past one, he heard a key turn in the lock, and his wife walked into the house. Bastien was overcome by emotion as he grabbed his wife, hugged her, and broke down into tears.

Gaea entered her parents' bedroom pulling Aerin by the hand. Vicky stood behind. "Tell them," Gaea demanded.

"Tell us what?" Bill asked. "You didn't do something else wrong, did you?"

"No, Daddy," Gaea said, pushing her brother closer to the bed. "Tell them."

"Daddy, I was wrong to go up onto the third floor. But there was this trap door in the bathroom, and I used my spy ring."

Bill rolled his eyes, and Cathy shushed her husband. "Go on." She urged.

"Well, I opened it and started to climb in, and I think it was the attic. I know I am not allowed to go near the attic, but I had to."

"You know that both the maid's quarters as well as the attic are off limits," Bill said, sitting up in the bed.

"I told the dork that," Vicky said, crossing her arms and leaning against the door frame.

"Vicky, your brother is not a dork." Cathy scolded.

"Fine. I will be in my room." She said, turned, and left.

"Tell them!" Gaea urged.

"I saw something up there," Aerin said softly.

Gaea pushed the boy aside and approached her parents. "He saw Jack, Daddy. He saw Jack in the attic."

CHAPTER 5
Kriegsmarine

No one got much sleep on either the Archaean Horizon or the Scion of the Seas. As soon as the sun broke to the east over the North Atlantic Ocean, both decks were abuzz with activity. The Portunus sat on the aft deck of the Scion as technicians made final system checks. An alarm went off, signaling the activation of the ship's crane as it moved slowly to hover over the deep-sea robot. Deckhands wearing hardhats guided the crane's drop lines and secured it to the Portunus. The Archaean Horizon was busy as well as they were preparing the Aquabot to dive in concert with Portunus. Even though it contained technology far inferior, the older robot still had its uses and was proving itself to be a valuable asset to the research team.

The nerve center for the dive was on the bridge of the Scion of the Seas, and all interested parties were present and accounted for. The respective captains were tasked with dealing with their respective ships' operations as well as maintaining a steady position throughout the dive. Both aquatic robots were tethered to their parent ship, and any drift by either boat could compromise the machines. Entanglement would spell disaster for the multi-million-dollar robots.

Tarpon and Brambilla stood with Dr. Laurent, overlooking the bank of monitors that would continuously show the data that both robots were collecting, including water temperature, salinity, and depth, in real-time. The Portunus was also equipped with the ability to collect water samples as it multitasked with its main mission. A second set of hi-resolution monitors broadcasted what the combined twelve cameras were recording on both robots. Both had high-powered lights, and with the addition of Aquabot, the team was hoping to illuminate the wreck enough to identify it.

"The problem is," Tarpon began, "is that a lot of the German U-boats did not have hull numbers painted on them."

"Yes," Brambilla added. "Quite clever if one stops to think about it. Identification of a vessel was essential for the Allies during World War II. The Germans ran some of their submarines in wolfpacks. If one were to be sunk or captured, the Kriegsmarine did not wish for the boat to be easily identified."

"How will we identify this one?" a technician attending to one of the computer stations asked.

"U-boats proudly displayed a coat of arms, if you will," Tarpon said. "Some were simple and some complex. I am hoping to find this crest if there is no hull number." Another alarm sounded, and the Portunus splashed into the ocean.

"Let the game begin," Brambilla said.

"Bill, how can this be possible?" Cathy asked, pouring herself a cup of coffee.

"I don't know."

"So, every person that dies in or near this house moves into our attic. It does not make sense. I am not happy, Bill."

"And you think I am?"

"What are we going to do? Now I feel guilty about grounding Aerin."

"Clarissa is supposed to stop by this afternoon. She knows a lot about these things. Maybe she will have some ideas." Bill offered.

"What about Aerin?"

"I'll have the old father and son talk and let him off the hook. I think he has learned a lesson."

"The girls are going to be pissed." Cathy reminded him. "You know how they are. They are going to bitch like hell claiming favoritism."

"If you talk to Gaea, I think she will be okay with it. It seems that her brother has her gift."

"I will talk to the girls, but dammit all if our son is a sensitive as well."

Bill finished off his coffee and stood up as his phone rang. "Hello?" Cathy looked at her husband curiously as he talked in broken and half sentences. "OK, but…why didn't you call her…OK…hold on." Bill handed his phone to his wife. "It's Dr. Bastien from the museum."

Gaea was clearly upset by what her brother claimed he had seen in the attic. She spent the better half an hour with him in his room, grilling him on what he thought he had seen. "Are you sure it was a man with red hair?" She asked him again.

"I keep telling you, yes. Clown hair but not as bushy. And he had freckles."

Gaea put her head in her hands and groaned. The psychic connection had been extremely strong between her and Jack Jefferson. That power had allowed them to defeat the demon Belphegor but at the cost of Jack's life. Now, she wondered if the connection had been so strong that he had become trapped here at the manor as Tracy had become. Rebecca remained a mystery to her. There was no reason why the spirit of the girl would remain behind. As far as Gaea knew, both Wilbur and his wife Lily had found peace and moved on. Why not her? She looked at her brother, who was nearly in tears. Pulling him to her, she hugged him and stroked his hair.

"I am sorry, Aerin. I really am." She whispered.

"It's not fair." He said through sniffles. "I'm sorry that I messed up."

"I'll talk to Mom and Dad, OK? I don't think it is fair either."

"I promise I won't go near the attic again."

Gaea thought to herself and looked up at the ceiling, "That, my dear brother, may not be a promise you can keep."

Bill had arrived at his son's open bedroom door as his daughter was embracing him. The sight warmed his heart. He tapped quietly on the door announcing his presence. Gaea looked up at her father and smiled. "Hi, Dad."

"Mind if I have a word with my son?" He asked, smiling.

"All yours." She said, standing up. Kissing Aerin's forehead, she left.

The dual undersea robots were working flawlessly. They seemed to dance together in harmony along the bottom of the North Atlantic at nearly seven hundred and seventy-five meters below the surface. The lights of the two submersibles penetrated the darkness illuminating the ocean floor beautifully. It did not take long before the aft section of the submarine appeared through the silt.

"My God, she is intact," Tarpon remarked.

"At least the ass end of it is," Brambilla commented. "Let us not get ahead of ourselves. There is more to examine. We will see what the rest of it looks like."

"Agreed," Jeffrey said.

The trio's eyes were glued to the monitor as more of the submarine was revealed. It lay on its belly as if it had been placed there; still, there was no sign of damage. It seemed to Tarpon as though the captain had simply intended to bottom his vessel, as was the practice for submarines of the day to avoid its enemy's sonar and depth charges. No captain would do such a thing at this depth.

"Not possible," Brambilla said. "There is no explanation for this boat to be in this condition at this depth. The crush depth of a U-bout was two hundred twenty meters. This thing should look like an aluminum can that has been run over by a tank."

Tarpon scratched the stubble on his chin and whispered to himself, "Unless..."

"All restrictions lifted for the convicted," Bill said to his wife as he entered the kitchen. "Except for no desserts for two weeks." Cathy did not seem to notice him. She was sitting down and did not appear to be herself. Bill looked down and saw his cell phone smashed on the floor. "Honey, what the hell?"

She looked up at her husband. "It is not possible. It is not God damned possible!"

Bastien was back in his office, and he refused to unlock the lab door—not until Dr. Pender arrived. The item that sat within was nothing to be toyed with, and he knew it. He wasn't sure if it was the same artifact that he had examined years before, but it looked identical to the one that had been possessed by a demon, and it made him nervous.

Jean-Claude Bastien was not a man of the cloth, nor did he believe in such, but what he had privy to was nothing less than terrifying. And when people died, it made a man take notice. The events at Shaw Manor that had been told had terrified his wife and shaken him as well. Denise did not believe the stories of the accident, and he did not buy into it either. Bastien and his wife had visited Shaw Manor numerous times, and he felt ill at ease every time. Something was not right with the house, but he could not put his finger on it. Denise was adamant. There was something evil that resided in the old manor. Dr. Bastien drank another shot of whiskey. He was alone on a Sunday and did not feel at ease.

"There it is." Jeffrey Tarpon said, pointing at the monitor. "See it?"

It had been hours of tedious inspection by the Aquabot and the Portunus. It was day three of the expedition, and every part of the wreckage remained, excluding the conning tower and the surrounding debris field. Surprisingly, there was no wreckage surrounding the U-boat. There was the expected rusting metal that had fallen in bits and pieces from the forward railings. For the most part, the submarine was intact and in immaculate condition. As the camera of the Aquabot passed across the conning tower, a crest was revealed. It looked to the scientists like the talon of a raptor on a yellow background.

"I give to you, my colleagues, the proof of identity of our submarine. This is the U-116 lost under the command of Oberleutnant zur See Wilhelm Grimme, last heard from on the 6th of October 1942. Spectacular."

"You are certain, Jeffrey?" Brambilla asked.

"There can be no doubt. Only one U-Boat had that symbol, and it was the U-116."

"I must agree."

"We have it identified. Now our work begins."

I am going to go over to the museum." Cathy informed her husband.

"Honey, my phone," Bill said, showing her the shattered glass of the iPhone.

"Screw your phone. Buy a new one." She said scornfully. "Get your keys. You are going with me."

"Why?"

Cathy started to cry, and Bill went to hold her. His wife was a strong woman but only so tough. He had learned over their years of marriage that certain things could break her. Something was not right, and he was not going to let his wife go at it alone.

"There is another ghost in the attic," Gaea said.

Vicky had been using her iPad to research recipes when her sister hit her with the news. The girl was convinced that she lived in a haunted house and that her sister had special abilities to know this. She had long abandoned the belief that she had such abilities. Her sister Gaea had them as well as her adopted mom. It was one of the reasons she loved to visit the Peppers up in Bar Harbor. The girl was grateful for being adopted by the Penders and loved her new sister; however, the house was creepy. Luckily, Gaea made her feel safe, and she knew she always had her best friend and sister by her side.

"So, what is new?" Vicky asked, feigning her fear.

"This could be nothing, Vicky. I am glad you are going up to the Pepper's."

Vicky put down her pad and went to Gaea to hug her. "For once, I would like to be here when these problems come up. I am a member of this family too."

"Aerin thought he saw something in the attic. It's probably nothing. He is a kid."

"He is like you, Gaea. I'm not like that. Sometimes I don't think I belong."

"But you do!" Gaea countered. "You are my sister!" Vicky looked at her with doubt.

"Look, I think of Bobby and Dottie Pepper as my grandpa and grandma. I know they are not, but I never knew mine. Sometimes we must take what is given to us. You have a new mom and dad. C'mon, sis."

"So, what is up?"

"Remember Jack?"

"You mean the nerdy writer kid?" Vicky asked.

"Okay, if you want to call him that. He was a really cool guy." Gaea replied.

"I really didn't know him much. Just from Dad's book thing. I knew Jeremy better."

"He was cool, too. Look, there are some strange things here at the manor. We both know that, but I don't think that it's anything bad, OK?"

"Okay," Vicky replied weakly.

"So back when we were kids, you remember when you were having a hard time with math?"

"Yes."

"Well, look at you now. I cannot figure out all the measurements that you use when cooking. And your dishes are delish!"

"Really? You like what I cook?"

"Are you kidding me? Even Mrs. Douglas is jealous."

Vicky laughed and hugged Gaea. "You have always made me feel special."

"You are. You are my sister." Gaea said, hugging Vicky back.

CHAPTER 6
Where There is Smoke

Dr. Jeffrey Tarpon had been contemplating the fate of U-Boat 116 for three days. The documenting of the wreck was going smoothly, however there was no evident cause of the sinking. The boat's hull had no signs of a breach, and apart from the rust, it seemed that it could be raised and put back into service. Tarpon was not the only one that was confounded by the condition of the find. Dr. Roland Brambilla was equally perplexed. "You think what?" Brambilla asked.

The two scientists had finally found time to be together privately and get away from the unrelenting demand of their research. Tarpon had chosen to get off the Scion of the Seas and spend the night on the Archaean Horizon with Roli. Every wreck that the team discovered seemed to open a Pandora's box of questions that led to more questions. This one seemed to be the granddaddy of all mysteries.

"Think about it." Tarpon began. "How can a U-Boat from World War Two sink to the bottom of the North Atlantic and remain intact? No apparent damage from an enemy ship. No evidence that it ran into an iceberg. It is like the captain simply brought it down and set it gently on the ocean floor. How and why?"

"You are postulating that Captain Wilhelm Grimme scuttled his boat, aren't you? I must admit that would answer some questions, but why would he do such a thing?" Brambilla asked. "If you will indulge me for a moment, I think I have a hypothesis for this."

Tarpon smiled. Brambilla stood and paced back and forth within the berthing area. "Let us assume for a moment that the one sixteen was running from the British Navy. It was not a wolf pack boat. It was a mine layer, so it is likely that it was on patrol by itself."

"Correct."

"The boat only had forward torpedo tubes, and its records were not the best. Four tours and it had only one kill and damaged one British ship. But that would be enough to piss off the Brits."

"Enough maybe to send a destroyer after it?" Tarpon said, smiling. He was enjoying watching Roli ponder things in his mind.

"Very plausible, Jeffrey. If the destroyer had had an encounter with the U-116 and somehow did some minor damage to it, which is not yet evident to us, the chase would have been on. There are records of ships chasing subs for weeks. The Japanese were known to be relentless in chasing American submarines. They would even look for and find garbage that had been ejected into the sea using their torpedo tubes. It seems the Americans were not so good at weighing down their garbage."

"Where are you going with this?" Tarpon asked, feigning ignorance.

"Let us assume for a moment that there was a skirmish and the U-116 was damaged. Not enough to sink her, but enough to restrict her movement. The boat could only stay submerged for so long before having to surface to cycle its air supply and do other routine maintenance. Let us also assume that Captain Grimme was exceptional at evasion, as most mine-laying skippers were at the time. Taking his boat out into the North Atlantic would have been the proper choice."

"Run and hide." Jeff nodded in agreement.

"Precisely. But that destroyer was faster than the one sixteen and outgunned it, what? Ten to one? I think that the German U-boat was low on diesel fuel, and the captain had simply run out of options. The orders from Berlin at the time were not to be captured under any circumstances."

"So, he flooded the ship and scuttled it," Tarpon added.

"Nothing else makes sense," Brambilla said, sitting on the bed beside Tarpon. "If the boat was fully flooded before reaching crush depth, it could have simply sunk to the bottom."

"Your deductive skills are why I love you, Roli."

"Shut it. You're the one who produced the hypotheses. Now how do we prove it?"

"We go back down and look to see if the hatches of the ballast tanks are still open."

"That is something that we could have easily overlooked," Brambilla said excitedly.

"You need to do a little digging and find out where on this boat those openings would be."

"Tomorrow morning, OK?"

"Yes. Tomorrow."

Bill drove Cathy up to Wells as she did not seem in any condition to drive herself. For the entire drive, she was deep in thought and remained tight-lipped about why they were going to the museum. He was concerned as he drove, listening to his wife mumble to herself. His questioning of her led to her telling him to shut up and drive. At the same time Bill was pulling into the museum's parking lot, Robert Pepper received the call.

"Sir, it's under control, but there is a lot of damage. All the presses are shut down and still under a no-entry order by the New York Fire Department." Liz Aquaro explained to her boss. "Luckily, the corporate wasn't touched, and we are operating under somewhat normal conditions."

"I don't call having my presses shut down normal conditions, Liz." Robert Pepper said gruffly. "What is the damage?"

"I do not have a full report on this as we can't get into the area to evaluate. Hopefully, later today. I just have preliminary information from the fire chief. It appears that this all started during the graveyard shift back in the press area that is under construction. It spread to the ink room as well as the paper room. From what I understand, both fire doors were left open. No one was hurt."

Pepper shook his head. "Damn sloppy. But I am glad about that. Why didn't security pick that up? We have cameras all over the plant."

"The cameras for that area were in the process of being moved due to the construction. I had ordered security to have a roaming guard placed, but it seems that he was on break when the fire broke out." Aquaro explained.

"Time to replace that security company, Liz."

"Yes, sir."

"Stop with the sir crap, Liz. This is not your fault. You cannot be at the plant twenty-four seven."

"I know, Bob. I just feel responsible."

"Your job is not in jeopardy whatsoever. I do want to know the cause of this fire. If it was someone smoking back there, I want their ass in a sling."

"You and me both. But it could have been worse."

"How?"

"The fire sprinkler system was slated to be shut down in the area today."

"Construction again?" Pepper asked.

"Yes. I am having doubts concerning this contractor, Bob."

"We may have to reevaluate them as well."

"Hopefully, we will have some answers soon."

"Keep me informed, Liz. We need to get back up and running ASAP." Pepper hung up and rubbed his forehead. He could feel one hell of a headache coming on.

"It's the same one, Bill," Cathy said, staring at the statue of Anubis.

"I think so as well." Dr. Bastien said, handing a half dozen photographs to him. "I took these when Denise brought the statue here to be evaluated."

Bill looked through them quickly and handed them to his wife. "I do not know squat about these things. I do know that the statue that was at the manor took an awfully long tumble down to the rocks and the Atlantic Ocean. I find it hard to believe that a piece of baked clay could sustain such an impact."

"Where did the lobsterman say he found it?" Cathy asked.

"He did not give me the coordinates but did say he was driving up from York Harbor. Lobstermen tend to drop their strings fairly close to home so I am guessing close to there."

"That is not very far from Cape Neddick," Bill noted. "But still, the fall that it took."

"What if it did survive the fall? Jack was holding the damn thing. Maybe he took the brunt of the fall, and somehow it missed the rocks?" Cathy surmised as she poured over the photos.

"I wasn't there," Bastien said. "But if it did make it intact into the open ocean it is conceivable that it could have drifted to wherever that lobsterman hauled it up."

Cathy gave all the photos to Bastien except one. Walking closer to the statue, she compared a portion of the head to the photograph in her hand. "It is the same statue. Look at this, " she said, pointing to a spot on the shoulder of the statue.

Bastien stepped forward, taking a magnifying glass from a table. "Well, I'll be damned. I missed that. You do have an eye, Dr. Pender." He said, peering through the glass.

"What?" Bill asked.

"Here, Bill. See that tiny chip on the shoulder of the statue?"

"I see it." He replied, taking the glass. "So what?"

"Now look at this photo," Cathy added, handing it to her husband. "Look close and tell me what you see."

"It looks the same," Bill answered.

"It is the same," Bastien commented. "Damn Cathy, how did you see that?"

"In my shop. I found that imperfection on my initial examination. That, as well as the issue of the short ears, is why I had reservations about it being a true Egyptian artifact and had Denise take it to you for a second opinion."

"There is no way that there could be an identical statue with the same mar on it," Bastien stated.

Bill stepped back, holding his hands up in defense. "That thing was possessed."

"Was." Bastien agreed. "I have seen no evidence that it is now." He pointed to a camera mounted to the ceiling. "I have had it under watch and locked up until now. It seems like a simple piece of baked clay."

"Seems," Cathy said. "I'm getting out of here now."

Dr. Bastien locked the lab door, and the three retreated to his office. "The question is, what do we do with the statue?"

"We?" Bill exclaimed. "We do not want anything to do with that thing."

"I was speaking metaphorically, Bill. It is in my possession."

"What are you suggesting, Dr. Bastien?"

"Crate it and send it to the Smithsonian. I have a couple of colleagues down in Washington who specialize in religious relics. One of them is a renowned parapsychologist."

"I didn't know the Smithsonian had a division that manages such things," Cathy remarked.

"Quite unknown except for a select few of us that have collaborated with them. They tend not to advertise such things. The research is valuable, and these scholars take items that have shown paranormal properties quite seriously. I think they will be extremely interested in this object."

"Better down there than here. There is no way in hell that it is coming near our house." Bill declared.

"Let's go," Cathy said, grabbing her husband's arm and pulling him toward the door.

"Thank you, Dr. Pender," Bastien called after them. "I got this. You can count on me."

Once they were in Bill's pickup, he looked at his wife. "Can we?"

"Can we what?" She answered.

"Trust him to get rid of that thing."

"I do trust him, Bill. He knows his stuff."

"I hope so. Let's go home."

Robert Pepper hung up his phone and went to talk to his wife. He had made the decision to fly back to New York and deal with the situation with his company. Dorothy would not be happy, but with the fire and Vicky driving up to visit, she would have to stay at the mansion. His pilot was already preparing his personal jet at Bangor International Airport, and all he had to do was pack an overnight bag and call for a car. Sometimes, Robert F. Pepper had to step in.

CHAPTER 7
A Sense of Presence

Dorothy Pepper was not entirely unhappy with her husband. She understood his concerns and always respected his wishes. When he told her of his plans to fly to New York to assess the damage to the publishing house, initially, she had wanted to accompany him. He argued that Vicky was coming up to visit, and the person she primarily wanted to see was Dottie. Thus, his wife easily relented as there was not much she could do. Years ago, Dorothy Pepper would have been making phone calls and organizing everything for Bob, including meetings with the police, the press, and the fire department. She was being honest with herself, deciding that she wanted nothing to do with the problem. Baking with Victoria was a much nicer choice.

Bob was not in such a positive attitude and had gone into what he called command mode. It took less than thirty minutes to inform all concerned that he was flying to New York City. Robert had procured a second corporate jet and had the older one rebuilt. The old jet was in a hangar on Long Island for use by the Pepper & Pepper executive staff, whereas the new jet was sitting at Bangor International Airport being fueled and prepped. He was packed and sat in the kitchen admiring his wife while waiting for a car to take him over to Bangor.

"Promise you will call me." She said, folding a dish towel. "A lot."

"Dottie, you are more important to me than this business. Of course, I will."

"Is it really worth it, Bobby?" She asked, walking over and sitting on his lap.

He looked at her and smiled weakly. "I am having my doubts. But it has been my life for decades. It can be hard to give up something so important."

"It was a big part of my life as well. I let it go. The moment you married me and took me to this wonderful place. And you let go of cigars and your scotch."

"Those were easy. I was hoping to just semi-retire and let others run the business. Everything was going so well."

Dorothy stroked her husband's hair and kissed him. "They still are. This is just a setback, nothing more. You will see when you get there." A horn honked outside. Bob kissed her cheek and slid her off his lap. He stood up and placed his day bag over his shoulder. Kissing her again, he turned and walked toward the front door.

"Honey?" She called after him.

"Yes?"

She pulled an envelope from her apron and handed it to her husband. It was open. "Tripod Publishing." He read the envelope aloud. "This is one of my competitors. When did this arrive?"

"Yesterday." She confessed. "I opened it and read it."

"Dorothy." He half scolded. "You are not my secretary anymore. What does it say?"

She smiled and pushed him toward the door. "Read it on the plane, OK?"

"Really, Vicky?" Gaea said, watching her sister load her Jeep for the drive up to Mt. Dessert Island.

"I might need this." She responded by taking the bag of flour from her sister's hands.

"And this salt, pepper, and vegetable oil? Grandma and Grandpa have this in their pantry."

"I don't want to deplete their supply. A good chef brings her own ingredients."

Gaea rolled her eyes, grabbed a bottle of fresh nutmeg from the box, and ran off. "Give me that back!" Vicky screeched, charging after her. After a short chase, the girls ran out on the lawn and fell onto the cold ground laughing. Panting, Vicky rolled over and stood up. Helping her sister up, she kissed her Gaea on her cheek. "I really love you."

"Me too," Gaea said, hugging her. "I'm going to miss you."

"It's only for the weekend."

"I know. Come on, let me help you finish packing."

Cathy felt better knowing that Dr. Bastien was going to send the statue of Anubis to the Smithsonian. The further away, the better. That evening she decided to talk to Gaea about the sighting of Jack up in the attic. Cathy had experienced no special feelings from any presence in the manor; Gaea, however, was much more in tune with her gift. Cathy found her daughter sitting on her bed, engrossed in a book; Piddles lay spread out next to her, snoring. "Hey honey, got a minute?" She asked.

"Sure, Mom," Gaea replied, placing a bookmark into the book and closing it. "What's up?"

Walking over, Cathy sat down on the bed. She picked up the book and read the title aloud, "*The Sensitive* by Dr. D. Dirkins. Is this helping?"

"Helping me to understand but not how to cope. I wish sometimes Rebecca and Tracy would just be quiet. And when I am out, the dead seem to come to me a lot. I tell them to leave me alone and most times they do. Some of them are aggressive, and I almost have to scream at them. It makes me feel terrible to do that. Mom, I just don't know how to ease their pain."

"It's not up to you to do that, Gaea. They have lived their lives, and for good or bad, it is over for them. You need to live your own life."

"I wish it were that easy. It is like a non-stop radio constantly playing inside of me, and I can't shut it off."

"When Clarissa is here next time, let's talk to her. She knows a lot of people who are familiar with this, and maybe we can get some help."

"I am afraid for Aerin as well. I think he has this ability." Gaea remarked.

"Speaking of your brother. What he says he saw up in the attic. I hate to ask, honey, but..."

"I have no feelings for Jack anywhere around me. I have not sensed him at all."

Cathy sighed and hugged her daughter before standing up to leave. "Maybe he saw Tracy."

"Mom, there is something else up there. I can sense it, but I am not sure what it is. It's not menacing, or at least I don't think it is. I am just not sure."

Robert Pepper stepped out of the elevator and onto the executive floor of his publishing house for the first time in nearly 8 years. Conference calls had kept the business running smoothly and in the black. He had no need to return. The fire had changed all of that, as did the letter that was tucked into his inner suit jacket pocket. Dorothy was still sly after all of the years, and she knew when to hold back something that could be extremely important. She was an expert at timing, and he knew it. Bob smiled and patted his chest and walked toward his old office.

Doors that led into offices lined both sides of the hallway that ran a thousand feet to a set of double doors which in turn led to his old office. He had made the walk from the elevator down the corridor countless times, and every time he had done so, he paused to look at the pictures of his grandfather and father that hung on the wall just outside the doors of the conference room. His picture hung next to them although he never thought much of it. "Too fat and way too smug." He said to himself.

It was still early when Bob entered the reception area of his office using his own pass key. Not much had changed except for the décor. Some paintings and a couple of plants, as well as the secretary's desk, were new. Crossing the room, he opened the door to his office. Immediately he was hit with the scent of lilac. It's not unpleasant, just unexpected.

He did not recognize the space. A new glass desk sat where his old one once was. A modern lumbar chair neatly pushed up behind it, along with two more that sat in front. His old wet bar and sofa were gone now and had been replaced with a new chaise lounge that looked extremely elegant. The artwork on the walls had a European flair and, to his curiosity, was not feminine. If Robert did not know who occupied the room, he could not have been able to guess if it was a man or a woman. He did think that the two small eureka palms were a nice touch considering Liz Aquaro's Puerto Rican heritage.

Bob walked to the large bank of windows and looked out over Manhattan. He had stood there thousands of times before contemplating decisions and pondering over things that, if it were not for Dottie, he thought he might have just lost his mind. If it had not been for Bill Pender, Robert F. Pepper might still be looking out at the steel jungle on a daily basis. His star writer's impromptu relocation up to Maine had started the gears turning in the printing mogul's mind. He had cooked up the idea of moving when his health came into question.

Talking with Clarissa about Maine, as well as his doctor's speaking about the state, had nagged at him for months. Looking at countless pictures of the coastline, pictures of Bill and his family enjoying their new manor had led him to contact a real estate agent. His plans to bring Dorothy along and ask her to marry him would be the frosting on the cake. If she refused, he surmised he would live there alone. His days of living in New York City were numbered. Bob was looking out the window one last time when he was interrupted by Liz Aquaro entering her office. He smiled and turned to greet her. "I'm sorry for letting myself in," he said. "A little nostalgia on my part."

"Not at all," Liz said, holding out her hand to greet her boss. "Your company, your prerogative to go where you wish."

"Not true," Pepper said, taking her hand for a brief shake. He walked to the front of the desk and sat in one of the two chairs. She took her seat of authority. "I have learned to respect what belongs to others, Liz. I am old. The way I used to do things is just not the way to do them in this day and age." Bob said, pulling the envelope from his pocket and handing it to her. "Read it."

"My pink slip?" She said, opening it half joking.

"If you lose your job, it will not be because of me."

She took a moment to read it before handing it back to him. "You're selling the company, " Liz said.

Pepper stood up and walked back to the windows. "A merger, if you will, " he said, turning to face her. I'm old, and I want time with my wife and without the stress."

"But you have that." She countered.

"Really? Do you think I wanted to have to come back to the city because of a fire?"

"I could have managed this easily, Bob. Look, we can go take a quick tour if you would like."

He shook his head and laughed. "You don't understand."

"I don't think I do."

"My grandfather founded Pepper and Pepper, and my father took it over. Then it became mine. When you love something so deeply, it becomes like a child, a well-protected one. I have no actual children, Liz. I never had time for it. This company has taken the majority of my life. If it were not for Dorothy, I would still be sitting in that chair where you sit now. I cannot take it anymore. I thought I could and was angry as hell at this fire. I wanted an ass in a sling and accountability. Then my wife handed me that letter as I was walking out the door and kissed me. It was on the jet flying down here that I realized what a fool I really am. I came to the realization that I don't need this publishing house to be happy. The company will live on without me. I made the right choice eight years ago to break away, but I just could not let go completely. I kept the leash in my hand and just didn't realize." Bob sat back down and looked at his general manager. "I am too tired for this shit."

She sighed and leaned back. "So, what is the plan?"

"The merger with Tripod will take time and I want nothing to do with it except when it is time for my signature. You are the leader of this company and will continue to function as such. I don't care about the damage, Liz. No lives were lost, and as far as the cause is concerned, that is up to you now. If there is liability, again your job. I know you will get this publishing house back up and running quickly. It is what you do, and you do it well. I am stepping down as the CEO and promoting you to the position. When it comes time for my signature send someone up to Maine for it. I am done. I have my stock in the company, so I have a say. I just don't want to be a decision-maker anymore. Understand now?"

"Without you, this company would not have become what it is."

"Perhaps, but without people like our writers and the simple folks downstairs, it would never have existed to begin with. The rest of us are just the duct tape that holds it all together."

"I do understand, Mr. Pepper, " she said, standing, walking around the desk, and hugging him. Thank you for trusting in me."

"Oh, stop it. I need to get back to Maine. My wife and granddaughter are cooking, and I need to get home."

"Bob, you said you have no children…"

"The child does not have to be blood to be family." He said and walked out the door.

Dorothy stood and watched as Vicky moved around her kitchen with the agility and talent of a well-trained ballet dancer. Her timing was exquisite as she prepped her various dishes, and as she prepared her meal, everything was perfect. "Grandma, please hand me the nutmeg for the custard. It will be done soon."

"I can do that, Vicky. You must let me do something to help."

Vicky paused and hugged the older woman. "I'm sorry. It's just that you have taught me so much and I wanted to cook for you and grandpa, and since he is coming home soon, I just thought..."

"Honey," Dottie said, "even a chef needs a sous chef."

CHAPTER 8
Growls

Clarissa and Bill sat at his desk in the widow's watch, going over the latest offer from Global Pictures. She knew of the tragedies that had occurred in the library but still she wondered about it. The room was simplistic in its beauty. She could easily understand why he wanted the space for himself. What did he call it? His Dreamer's Hideaway. It was a spectacular place to sit and weave tales. Bill stood up and poured himself a cup of coffee. "Refill?" He asked.

"No thanks." She replied, standing up and stretching. She walked to the open French doors that overlooked the Atlantic Ocean. She could hear the ocean smashing against the rocks nearly a hundred feet below.

"I'm glad that you brought Logan with you today. Aerin really likes your son." Bill said, sitting back down.

"His day school was canceled this week, so I figured it was a suitable time for the two of them to catch up. They are almost the same age."

"Aerin is seven, and Logan is six. Not much of a difference at that age."

"No, there isn't." Clare agreed. "It is kind of good timing as Doug is at a shrink symposium in New York."

"Oh?"

"He is being honored by his psychologist peers. Thanks to me having to help you finalize this deal I was able to squirm out of going. Those things are just too damn stuffy for my liking."

Bill laughed. "I can't say that I blame you for bailing. I used to try every excuse in the book to get out of those book signings and appearances that I used to have to go to."

"Speaking of books, Jack's final novel is hitting the shelves this week." She said somberly.

Bill sighed. "That kid had so much talent."

"Every one of his previous five novels have become best sellers and I am anticipating that so will this sixth."

"Thankfully, his genre is horror and not spy and intrigue. He might have buried me." Bill said with a slight laugh.

"I doubt that. Sometimes you don't give yourself enough credit for your own literary brilliance."

"Clare, Cathy wants to talk to you when you have time. It seems that Aerin got up into the maid's residence and found a hatch that allowed him to begin crawling into the attic. Luckily, Mrs. Douglas found him and yanked him back out."

"Adventurous little guy." She remarked.

"He is, and that is not all. He claims he saw something in the attic. A young man with red hair and freckles."

Clarissa's jaw dropped. "Jack? I cannot believe it. No, I take that back. With this house, anything is possible."

"It shook Aerin up, to say the least," Bill said, taking a sip of coffee.

"I can imagine. So how can I help?"

"It's Gaea. My daughter's abilities are gaining strength, and she is having problems controlling them. If Aerin is also sensitive, we need to start getting the boy's abilities under control as soon as possible. We are hoping you might have some ideas on this problem. Cathy is upset as well."

"Of course, Bill. I do have some ideas."

"One more thing Clare. The statue has resurfaced."

"We know where to look for those ballast openings." Dr. Brambilla said, sitting down next to Dr. Tarpon in the Scion of the Seas main galley. "It wasn't easy, but I had an old friend send me this drawing of the class of submarine that the U-116 is. She was a type XB minelayer." He said, placing the diagram on the table.

"It's not very detailed," Tarpon stated.

"Like I said, it was not easy. I came to find that there are few detailed diagrams left of nearly all the German U-boats. A lot of the top-secret documents from the area were destroyed before the allies could capture them."

"But this one tells us what we need to know?"

"I believe it does, Jeffrey. Look here." He pointed to the bow of the boat, then to the amidship, and finally the aft. "The main ballast ports are on the bottom of the boat and might be buried in the mud. However, the auxiliary ports are near the top of the submarine. For the U-116 to submerge, all of the ports have to be opened. The type XB, like all submarines, was equipped with compressed air systems. They are used to blow the water out of the ballast tanks when it surfaces. These are open when it dives. Only partially flooded ballasts are needed to make the boat submerge."

"I see, but this brings up another problem to the scuttling theory, doesn't it?" Tarpon asked, examining the document.

"Yes, it does. Flooding the ballast tanks would have caused the U-116 to sink like a rock, however..."

"She would still have air within the pressure hull, and once at crush depth, we should see massive damage to our boat." Tarpon broke in.

"It does, and we should unless we are missing something."

"Dammit. Well, let us start by finding these ballast ports first and keep looking. The robots are going down again in thirty minutes. Let's get breakfast and stuff our faces. We need to get up to the bridge. I have a feeling it's going to be a long day." Jeffrey said. Brambilla nodded.

Cathy, Clarissa, and Gaea sat on the sofa in the great room, talking over herbal tea. Aerin and Logan were outside playing, and Bill remained in his office writing. "I'm not overly concerned about the statue, Cathy," Clare said. "It could have survived the fall and simply washed out to sea. And you are saying that Bastian is sending it to the Smithsonian?"

"Yes." She answered.

"I am more concerned with what is happening in this house, particularly up in the attic. What are you feeling, Gaea?"

"I always sense Tracy and Rebecca, but there seems to be something else. I cannot place it. It's like whatever it is, it's hidden from me."

"And Aerin describes something that might be Jack. Strange. Your brother has never met Jack, Gaea, so how can he describe someone that he has never met?"

"He never mentioned a name to me," Cathy added.

"Nor me either."

"Gaea, what I am about to suggest you might not like." Clarissa began.

"You want me to go up into the attic." The girl said flatly.

"Not right this minute and not this week. I want to talk to Dr. Dirkins about this. It might be nothing more than a child's imagination, but I am not passing anything off. I have a friend who lives over in Ogunquit, and she is sensitive. Her name is Lillian, and she is older, so she has been dealing with what you are going through for many years. She can help you in controlling what the dead are throwing at you."

"I would like that," Gaea said, tears forming in her eyes. She wiped them with her sleeve and tried to compose herself. "No matter where I go, they come to me."

"I believe Lillian can help you to block them and control them so it will be more manageable."

"What about Aerin?" Gaea asked.

"I will ask her about him, but he is young. I think you need to get your abilities under control first, and then, as he grows older, you can help him. I am not an expert, mind you. Lillian will have more precise advice."

"There is something else," Aerin said. The three turned in surprise.

"Aerin!" Gaea exclaimed, motioning for her brother to come to her. He did and crawled up next to his sister.

"Honey, where is Logan?" Clarissa asked.

"Playing with Piddles outside. I told him I had to go to the bathroom."

"What do you mean there is something else?" Cathy asked.

"That man was there because I saw him. He had red hair and freckles on his face. He said my name."

"You told me that," Gaea said.

"There was another sound that came from behind him when Mrs. Douglas pulled me out. It was a woman's voice, and she growled at me." Cathy dropped her teacup on the rug.

Is that all, Aerin?" His sister asked. He nodded and wrapped his arms around her neck in a fierce hug. "Go play with Logan, 'K?" She asked. "We will talk later."

"OK." The boy said, jumping down and running toward the front door.

"It seems that we might have to visit the attic sooner than I previously thought," Clarissa said. "I am going to go call Dr. Dirkins."

"I smell something wonderful!" Bob Pepper shouted as he walked into his home. His wife and Vicky met him at the door, and Dottie hugged him.

"That was a short trip," Dottie said, kissing his cheek. "Talk about it?"

"Later, OK? Right now, I am starving."

"Grandpa!" Vicky exclaimed. It was her turn to hug him. "I hope you like it. Oh my gosh!" Vicky shouted and turned to run back to the kitchen.

"I'm sure I will never get used to being called that." He said, handing his bag to one of the mansion's staff. "But I like it."

"Me too." His wife said, kissing him again.

"How long until dinner?" He asked.

"About an hour."

"Good, then I have time to shower."

The staff of the Pepper mansion served the meal that Vicky and Dottie had prepared, allowing the three to sit and enjoy it. They had created a four-course meal that delighted Bob Pepper. "I have never had this. What is it?" Bob asked, digging into his salad.

"It is a fiddlehead fern salad with mint tossed in hickory nut oil with chives and a splash of fresh lemon juice," Vicky replied, taking a bite of her own.

"Fiddleheads?" He inquired.

"They are a natural plant here in Maine. They grow near brooks, rivers, and lakes during the spring after the winter snow melts. I love them." Vicky said. "Unfortunately, these are preserved from this spring and not fresh."

"They are splendid. Am I wrong, Dottie?"

"They are delicious." His wife stated.

The salad was followed by fresh crusty bread, which paired perfectly with the bowl of New England clam chowder. Bob could not eat enough of it and could hardly wait until the main course arrived. It consisted of roast pheasant served with onion and orange marmalade, fresh green beans, and wild mushrooms on the side.

"Vicky, where did you learn this?" Bob asked. "The finest restaurants in New York do not serve food this good."

She just beamed in response.

By the time the plates were cleared, Bob was stuffed and was not sure he could manage some heavy dessert. To his surprise, he was presented with a rather small cup that he recognized immediately. "Custard, " he said, smiling broadly. "My favorite. You have been conniving with my Dottie, haven't you, young lady?"

"Bobby, I admit I told her that it is your favorite, but this is her own recipe. She would not let me touch it. Well, except for grinding the nutmeg and sprinkling it on before it went into the refrigerator."

He put a spoonful into his mouth, and the look on his face was all Vicky needed to see. Robert Pepper was in food euphoria. "If your father does not set you up in your own restaurant, I will. It's simply spectacular. You outdid yourself."

"I knew you had to fly to the city to handle company business and when Grandma told me you were coming right home, I just wanted to make something special."

"It is special, Vicky. Beyond special. And about that company business. Dorothy, I have resigned as the CEO of the company, effective immediately. Liz is taking over. Time for me to let go." Dottie's eyes went wide, and she leaped into her husband's arms. Vicky clapped and cheered. "Oh, I have my stocks and will be a minor board member, but no more decision-making for me. Let the younger people manage it. I am done, Dottie. It's time for you and me and our other family members."

"I can't believe it. It's been so long in coming."

Vicky coughed and excused herself from the table. This was a moment that was Bob and Dottie's and not for her. "Thank you, Vicky!" Bob called after her. She waved and headed for the kitchen.

CHAPTER 9
Lillian

It did not take long for Clarissa to set up a meeting between Lillian and Gaea. The woman was more than excited to assist with the issue at hand. Gaea did not want to go alone so Bill offered to go along with his daughter. Cathy needed to go into the Kennebunk shop to take care of a few things. Gaea was clearly nervous as her dad drove the short distance from Cape Neddick up to Ogunquit. Lillian's instructions were simple enough. Drive to Perkins Cove, park, and walk up the Marginal Way. The third house is on the left. Walk through the gate and come up to the back porch.

Bill was familiar with the homes that lined the historic cliff walk that ran from the cove all the way north to Ogunquit. Most were large mansions; however, a few were quaint, well-cared-for homes. Some were larger than others, but all were spectacular in their own way and had incredible views of the Atlantic Ocean as well as of the rocky coastline of Maine. Bill had considered the area before Shaw Manor became known to him, and it was a deal he could not refuse. He had had some doubts about all of the happenstances that occurred. Nevertheless, the majority of the time he and his family had spent at the historic estate was peaceful and enjoyable and outnumbered the horrors that they had endured. Bill glanced at his daughter as he turned onto Perkins Cove Road. "Honey, don't be afraid. It is going to be fine." He reassured her.

"I'm not afraid." She answered. "I just don't know what to expect."

"It's going to be OK, baby." He said, pulling his pickup into an open parking space. Although the season was technically over, a few artists were gathered: painting and sketching the beauty before them.

Gaea opened the door, climbed out, and inhaled deeply, the cold salty air permeating her senses. "Why does it smell different here than at home?"

Bill shrugged, locking the truck. "It might be because this is a fishing village. Look at all the lobster traps stacked over there." He pointed at the traps. A man walked up, and Bill paid him the five-dollar parking fee.

"I guess." She took her dad's hand, and the two of them walked toward the beginning of the Marginal Way.

Lillian Shawn was nervous in her own right. Not about dealing with the paranormal and another sensitive as Clarissa had explained to her over the phone, but that Bill Pender and his daughter were coming to see her, and she did not do well with famous people. Especially if it was her favorite writer. Having knowledge of certain things that he may or may not want a person to know troubled the woman. She was a straightforward woman, and when it came to advising clients, she refused to sugarcoat anything. She was compassionate but would not lie or fabricate fairy tales to ease their pain or discomfort. Things were what they were, and that was that.

Lillian had just set a tray of warm blueberry muffins onto a table that dominated the right side of the closed-in veranda, which, in her opinion, had the best view of the ocean and the harbor when the back gate buzzer sounded. "Yes?" She said into the intercom.

"The Penders here to see Lillian."

"I'll buzz you in." She replied and looked down the yard toward the Marginal Way. She watched as the two entered and closed the gate behind them. She waved, and they waved back, walking up the path that led to the house. "Hello," Lillian said as the two walked up onto the veranda. "Welcome to my humble abode. Please sit down. I have coffee, tea, and fresh muffins while we chat. I am Lillian. Lillian Shawn. But you can call me Lily."

Bill sat down and looked at the woman. "We have met before."

Lily picked up the pot of tea. "Tea?" She asked Gaea, ignoring his statement.

Gaea smiled. "The muffins smell delish, and yes, please!"

She poured the tea and looked at Bill, offering him some as well. He waved her off. "Coffee, please."

Lillian sat back and helped herself to a muffin. "Help yourself, Mr. Pender."

"Bill. Please call me Bill, and this is Gaea, my daughter."

"Hello, my dear."

"Hello," Gaea said, taking a small bite.

"Before we get started," Lily began, "Yes, we have met. It was a long time ago and only for a moment."

"The grocery store," Bill said, putting a small amount of cream into his coffee.

"I am surprised that you remember," Lily said, sipping her tea.

"You startled me because I thought you looked like someone."

"Lily Shaw."

"Well, yes." He responded, stunned. "How…"

"Lily Shaw was my great-grandaunt." She spoke matter of factly. Bill nearly dropped his cup into his lap, and Gaea looked up from her partially eaten muffin. The woman laughed and set her cup down. "It's not so dramatic as one might think. I know of Wilbur and Lily and of the tragedies that befell them. And as far as I know, the two sisters were never close. They were twins, did you know that? But of course, you wouldn't. Not much was written down about the history of the Shawn family. The Shaw family, yes, because of Wilbur's father."

"This is all new to me, Lillian." He spoke.

"Wilbur did not make the money to build that house you currently live in through fishing. His father, Jonas, was a textile baron and made a fortune in the early 1800's. When he died, Wilbur sold the company and went to his love."

"The sea." Bill commented.

"Yes, and it seems that he was quite successful at it."

"Did you know that Lily Shaw had a daughter?" Bill blurted out. Lillian dropped her cup onto the table.

Cathy wrapped things up quickly with Denise at her side. A few expensive antiques needed authentication signatures which took them both to complete. "This step used to be a pain," Cathy stated. "It's why I used to send you over to Dr. Bastien. Now, with your degree, you can authenticate a lot of these things."

"My husband still helps out when you aren't around. I would have called on him for this, but he is busy at the museum."

"Oh, yes. How is it going with that damned thing?" Cathy asked, sitting down.

"He's got it created, and hopefully, later today, Anubis, or whatever it is, will be on its way south."

"Not a minute too soon."

"I am so sorry about what you went through, and I can't believe that it just showed up all of a sudden," Denise said sympathetically.

"It was a long time ago. It was just surprising when that fisherman dropped it off at the museum."

"Surprising?" Denise exclaimed. "My husband was traumatized. I was up in Bangor. I came home to a blabbering fool!"

"I know, and I am sorry. Bill took me up to Story Land for the day. We did not even think of answering our phones."

"I would not have either. I can admit that. I love that place. My parents took me there every summer. So magical."

Cathy smiled. "It brought back a lot of memories for me."

"I can imagine."

"I used to go there with a cousin when we were both really young. I wish I were still in touch with the little brat."

"Why can't you?" Denise asked.

"The last time I knew, his family was up in Canada. Montreal, I think."

"And there is no way to try and track him down? C'mon, Dr. Pender, it is one thing at which you are particularly good."

Cathy laughed. "Maybe. I just have not had the time to even try. I would not even know where to begin."

"Hey, why not let me give it a go?" Denise asked. "I studied genealogy for a semester at university. I really think I can help, and it would be fun."

"You really want to do this?" Cathy asked skeptically.

"I do! Please let me." Denise pleaded.

"OK, but on your own time. So, what do you need from me?"

After getting over the shock of finding out she had another lost relative and Bill promising to show her the family cemetery, Lillian Shawn was ready to talk about the primary reason the Penders were at her home. "First of all," Lillian said, "Gaea is not a sensitive. She is a medium."

"What does that mean?" The girl asked.

"It means, my dear child, that you have the rare ability to communicate with the dead, and you attract them like a moth to a flame."

"I don't like it. I do not like it at all." Gaea replied.

"And there is no cure for this disease thing?" Bill asked.

"Our gift is not a disease, William. Why are we given this ability? I have no idea and do not know anyone who does." She turned her attention to the girl. "Gaea, it is a wonderful gift, but it can be terrifying. This fact I know."

"I am afraid, and they won't leave me alone."

Lillian sighed and took Gaea's hand into hers. "There are things we can do to make the situation better."

"Like what?" She asked. Bill sat back in his chair, feeling helpless.

"First of all, we have to take control of every situation that we find ourselves in."

"How?"

"One way to go about it, that I use daily, I like to call the charismatic shield. It is a technique that you will use with your mind. It will allow you to block unwanted spirits from invading and trying to take over your personal space. Do you understand?"

"I think so. I just don't know how."

"That is why you are here, right?" Lillian asked. Gaea nodded in affirmation. "Good," Lillian said, closing her eyes. Bill watched as his daughter closed hers as well.

Some time passed as they seemed locked in some sort of connection that he had not witnessed since Gaea had done something similar with Jack. It made him nervous, but he held his tongue and fidgeted in his seat. With no sounds emanating from the two, it made the time more unbearable. Finally, Lily's eyes popped open, and she released Gaea's hand. Standing up, she went into the house. The girl opened her eyes as well and sat motionless, staring at the table. "Are you OK, baby?" Bill asked his daughter. She simply looked up at him.

Bill charged into the house, looking for Lily, and found her sitting on a chair with her eyes closed. "What the hell did you do to her?!" He demanded. The woman's lips moved, but he could hear nothing. Leaning forward, he put his ear near her mouth and asked again. "What did you do to her?"

Lillian opened her eyes. "Gaea is much more than a medium she whispered. She has fought evil and has won. At least for now."

"What are you talking about?"

"I could see it."

"See what?" Bill asked.

"The battle. Gaea may have fought the devil himself." Bill stumbled back and fell onto a couch. "The battle is not over." She said. "I must go to the manor."

As Bill drove Gaea back to Shaw Manor, she was mostly silent until they neared the entrance to the estate. "Baby, please talk to me." Bill pleaded.

Gaea looked at him. "I understand now, Daddy. It was somehow like when I was with Jack, except he was much stronger than Lillian. But she was able to show me. I know how to do the charismatic shield. I think that that was what Jack was trying to show me but didn't have time before, well, you know."

"What did she mean the battle is not over?"

"I'm not sure," Gaea said, returning to more of her normal state of mind. "Maybe it is me dealing with the dead."

"I hope so, Gaea," Bill said, but he was not so sure.

CHAPTER 10
A Catastrophe & A Kitten

The bright lights of the Aquabot and the Portunus cut through the darkness. However, silt partially obscured their cameras as they glided slowly over the black hull of the German U-boat. The morning goal was clear but could take some time—perhaps not completed in a single dive. The objective was to locate and verify if the ports for the ballast tanks had been opened or closed when the sub sank. Dr. Jeffrey Tarpon was betting on finding them open. The ever-skeptical Dr. Brambilla was not so confident.

"Portunus is coming up on the aft starboard ballast port," Tarpon said, staring at the monitor. "We should see it soon. To submerge, it must be open, along with the main port, which is below and, unfortunately, buried in the mud. But if the auxiliary ports are open, then it is enough to logically assume that the mains are open as well."

"I don't like to assume anything, but in this case, I must agree with you. The only time the auxiliary ports are opened is when the ballast tanks are being flooded. Damn this mud and silt." Brambilla added. "It is so fine it becomes unsettled if the smallest of sea creatures passes by."

"Look, Roli!" Tarpon exclaimed. Brambilla leaned forward, and out of the gloom, he could make out what appeared to be a port. It was open.

Cathy had returned home an hour before Bill and Gaea. Although she was worried sick about how it was going with their meeting with the medium, she was passing the time watching Aerin and Logan run around the front lawn of the estate. Both boys were bundled up due to the chilly fall air. With Clarissa having some extra work on her hands and Logan not being at day school, the two boys had a ton of time to play together. So far, the boy had practically moved in for the week and it had taken some strain off from Cathy as well as the house staff. Having promoted, Denise had been a major relief as well. Not having to deal with the day-to-day operations of her shops gave her more time for her children as well as her husband.

She sat in a Cape Cod chair and watched the two, Piddles at her feet, snoring contently. The Boxer had worn herself out with the boys earlier and now lay sleeping with her tongue hanging partially out of her mouth. Cathy was absentmindedly lightly scratching her behind her ears when the dog suddenly sat up. "What is it?" Cathy asked the boxer, who simply looked at her. A moment later, Bill pulled up and parked his truck close to the front door. "Of course. Come on, Piddles, let's go greet Daddy and Gaea."

The boys had already charged toward the truck and Bill had picked up his son and was walking towards Cathy. Piddles attacked Gaea with more kisses than the girl seemed to want. Pushing the dog away, she made her way into the manor without so much as a word to her mother.

"We need to talk," Bill said, kissing his wife.

The weekend had flown by, and before she knew it, Vicky was saying goodbye to Bob and Dottie Pepper. Visiting her "adopted" grandparents was one of her favorite things in life. As a young child, she had never really known or had a family. Now, she was a Pender with a real mom and dad as well as a brother and a sister.

When she was introduced to the Peppers, it just seemed natural to call them her grandparents. She knew they were not actually her grandma and grandpa, but it just seemed to fit, and it felt natural. It always made her sad when she left to head back to Cape Neddick. But the thought of seeing her family was the kicker.

As she drove off Mt. Dessert Island, she whistled happily to a song on the radio. Then she saw the sign and pulled over. A handwritten sign that was attached to a tree simply read *kittens*. Vicky turned off her Jeep and climbed out. It was a small house that was set back from the road. There was no telephone number written on the sign, so she walked up the driveway and was met by an old woman, her face wrinkled and her hair scraggly and gray. "I saw the sign," Vicky said.

"Well, of course you did. Would you like to meet the kittens? They are quite lovely."

"Yes, ma'am, I would. Very much!"

"Come then, they are over here in a box."

Vicky could not believe her eyes as she gazed into the box. The kittens were tiny and each one had multicolored fur except for one that was nearly pure white except for a spot of brown on its back. It looked up at her and mewed. Something else took her aback, and she had to look twice. The cat had two different colored eyes. One blue and the other, although still in the process of changing, she could tell it would be brown. "Chimer," Vicky whispered.

"What, dear?" The woman asked.

"Oh, nothing. Can I take this one?"

"Yes. Twenty dollars, please. It helps me to feed and take care of the rest of the lot. They weren't mine to begin with. Someone dropped them off in my yard. I could not bear to see the poor little things suffer." Vicky opened her purse, found a twenty-dollar bill, and handed it to the woman. "Enjoy!" The woman said and walked toward the house.

Vicky cradled the kitten in the crook of her arm as she opened the hatch of the Jeep. She had kept the boxes she had used to bring up her supplies and reaching for a towel; she quickly made a temporary bed inside the deep box. "I don't think you can climb out of this," Vicky said placing the kitten into its temporary home. She rubbed it behind its ears, and to her surprise, it yawned, stretched, and went to sleep. She closed the door gently and got back on the road. Hopefully, her mom would like the gift she had just adopted and intended to give to her.

Cheers erupted on the bridge of the Scion of the Seas. The final port had been located, and all the ports showed signs of being open. A substantial portion of the hypothesis seemed to be true. Still, it was troubling to the two scientists. There was still no evidence that the submarine had suffered catastrophic damage upon reaching its crush depth which was a maximum of two hundred and twenty meters. The U-116 was lying at a depth of seven hundred and seventy-five meters.

Tarpon called the mission for the day as it would take time to recover the two mini-subs, and they would need to go through their routine maintenance checks before their next dive. There was also a ton of footage to review and analyze from the day's activities. Tarpon and Brambilla left the recovery efforts to the respective ship captains and the crew. "Celebratory dinner in the officer's mess?" Jeffrey suggested.

"That sounds good to me," Roli replied. "I could go for a glass of red wine, and we need to start thinking about the problem with our theory."

"I have an idea or two."

"I hope you do because my idea factory seems to have shut down."

Tarpon laughed and put his arm around Brambilla's shoulders. "Let's go eat."

The boys had settled down with a bowl of popcorn and watched the cartoon channel with Piddles lying at their feet. Cathy, Gaea, and Bill sat in the kitchen and talked quietly. "Tell me what happened," Cathy said, passing the carafe of coffee to her husband.

"Dad, tell her about Lillian," Gaea spoke to her father.

"You are not going to believe this." He began. "Lillian Shawn is a blood relative of Lily Shaw."

"No way."

Bill nodded. "Lily was Lillian's great-grandaunt. Lily Shaw had a twin sister, but according to her, the women did not get along and never spoke. She was also quite taken aback to learn about Rebecca."

"What about you, Gaea? That is why you went; to see a sensitive and get answers." Cathy asked her daughter.

"She is not a sensitive, Mom. And neither am I. Lillian thinks that she and I are mediums."

"You can communicate with the dead," Cathy stated. "I do know what a medium is. How does that make you feel?"

Gaea shrugged and stared at the table. "I guess I already knew. Jack was one as well."

"Lillian showed Gaea how to do something to help shield herself from the dead, didn't she honey?"

Gaea looked up at her mother. "She called it a charismatic shield and I can do it. I used it on the way back from her house. I think that Jack had tried to teach me how to as well, but I was too young to understand, and he didn't have the time to explain it. Lillian took her time, and it seemed so simple to perform."

"What is it?" Her mother asked.

"It is a state of my mind that I put myself into. The best way I can explain it is that I imagine a wall of energy that surrounds me. A happy energy. For me, it is light powder blue in color. The dead appear to be held back by it, and I cannot hear them."

Cathy nodded. "Powder blue has always been your favorite color. Maybe that has something to do with it?"

"Maybe. Lillian didn't tell me what color hers is. I am happy it works."

"There is more," Bill said.

"Tell me."

"Lillian wants to come here."

"Why?"

"She is concerned about what is in the attic. Not Rebecca or Tracy but of whatever else is up there."

Cathy lowered her head into her hands. "Bill, that statue is on its way out of state."

"It's not the statue anymore, Mom," Gaea said. "There is something else, and it is not Jack."

The three were interrupted just then by Vicky coming in the front door. "I'm home!" She called.

"Yay!" Aerin cried and ran towards his sister.

"We will talk more later, OK?" Gaea asked. Her father and mother nodded their assent and the three stood up to go greet Vicky.

Vicky had set down her overnight bag and a basket she had bought on her way home. Piddles had already discovered the contents within the wicker container and sniffed at it obsessively. "Stop that." Vicky scolded, trying to shoo the dog away.

"Brought some goodies home?" Bill asked while watching the Boxer.

The girl hugged her family and sighed, picking up the basket. She handed it to her mom and said, "I hope you like it." Cathy looked at her daughter skeptically. Before she could pull the towel aside, the kitten poked its head out and mewed. She took one look at it and started to cry. "Mom, I'm sorry!" Vicky exclaimed. "I wanted you to be happy."

"I am happy," Cathy said, pulling the cat from the basket. "He looks like Chimer, and he is adorable. Where did you get him?"

"There was a sign on a tree not far from Grandpa and Grandma's house. I stopped and saw this one and I thought he looked just like Chimer as well. Look at his eyes, Mom."

"He has the same genetic feature. Heterochromia. I can see it." Cathy said, reaching out to hug her adopted daughter.

"Pretty cool, Vicky. Very cool." Gaea said.

"Let's just hope Piddles doesn't eat it," Bill said jokingly.

"Jerk," Cathy replied. "What's his name?"

"He doesn't have one. The kitten was left in a woman's yard along with the rest of the litter."

Cathy thought for a moment and placed the kitten on the floor, where Piddles began to sniff and lick the new addition to the household. Within a few moments, the dog was on its back, and the cat was crawling all over the Boxer, licking it with his tiny tongue. The two boys laughed hysterically. "I was wrong," Bill said, laughing. "The cat is going to eat the dog."

"I know," Cathy said, "Lick. Yup, that is the kitten's name."

Bill rolled his eyes. "Really?"

"I love it!" Gaea exclaimed. "It is perfect. C'mon, Dad, you always told me that characters should be named as they act. Especially animal characters."

"That's right," Vicky said. "That is how Piddles got her name!"

"You remember that, huh?" Bill asked.

"I remember everything you tell me, Daddy," Gaea replied, hugging her father.

"What about food for our new liability?" Bill said, smiling.

"It is in my Jeep, along with a new kitty box and a bag of litter. He is too young to go outside yet."

"You are clever," Bill admitted.

"She is my sister," Gaea added.

"Oh, by the way, Dad, Grandpa is selling his business."

Bill's face turned ashen.

CHAPTER 11
Ethereal Under the Pines

Professor Ian McCloud received the shipment from Dr. Bastien late in the afternoon. Interns working for the paranormal research wing of the Smithsonian's Department of Oddities unpacked the crate and moved the statue to a lab table. "What do you think, Professor? " a young man asked, stepping back from it.

"It is intended to be Anubis, the Egyptian God of the underworld." He responded by running his hand through what remained of his white hair. Removing his glasses, McCloud cleaned the lenses and placed them back on his face. "But it is not correct. Too many things are not right with it."

"So, it is a fake?"

"Fake, Mathew? I would not make that assumption so quickly. Being a fake would mean an intent to defraud. I do not think that is the case here. It is not a correct representation of Anubis, which is clear to me. Perhaps it was not intended to be as such. Thus, that raises the question, what is it, and for what was it made? And that, my boy, is why Dr. Bastien has sent it to us."

Mathew nodded. "Where would you like me to start, Professor?"

"Pictures and measurements, of course. Then, we shall examine its composition and the painting and hopefully place it in history. A proper date will take us far in the identification of the statue."

"I will get on it."

"And Mathew?"

"Yes, sir?"

"Ask Madeline to start doing the book research. She is incredibly good at pouring through printed literature as well as the internet. We might just find our friend here listed in our own archives."

"Got it," Mathew said and left the professor alone.

McCloud looked over the onyx statue closely. "What are you? Who are you?" He murmured.

"I can't believe he is actually selling Pepper & Pepper Publishing, Clare," Bill said to his agent over the phone. "Who to?"

"From what I know, Tripod made an offer and part of his decision was simply he is over it and wants to spend time with his wife as well as your kids, Bill. Both he and Dorothy adore Vicky and Gaea. I think the fire was the kicker, however. He is in his seventies."

"Yeah, and I know how much my two daughters mean to them, especially Vicky. The girls feel the same about Bob and Dottie. What does it mean for me?"

"Nothing. Your contract is as solid as it is. And if they want to renegotiate it, they will risk losing you to a competitor. You hold all the cards, Bill."

"That's good to know." Bill took a few minutes and filled Clarissa in on what had transpired with Lillian Shawn.

"So, your daughter is a medium. I suspected as much, but I do not believe that Cathy has that ability. She is a sensitive."

"What is the difference?" Bill asked.

"Night and day. Cathy can sense things and, from time to time, can see a spirit but not communicate with it. Gaea can speak to the dead."

"I wonder why the difference?"

"Sometimes the gift skips a generation, or in some cases, only limited ability is inherited."

"Lillian taught Gaea some kind of shielding technique to help her with coping with dealing with the deceased. A charismatic shield."

"I have heard of it. Different people call it different things, but it is the same for all mediums. I don't know too much about it. Doug knows more than I do. He has been doing a lot more in the field since he got his doctorate in parapsychology."

"Yeah, it was interesting that he went into that right after what happened to us up here in my office," Bill stated.

"It was the catalyst that pushed him into doing it, although he has always had an interest," Clare replied.

"What do you think about the three of you coming for dinner soon?" Bill asked. "When Doug gets back? We would love to have you."

"That would be wonderful! Logan has been overjoyed going over to the manor and visiting with Aerin. I am thinking about nixing the idea of the private day school thing altogether. The only reason we did it was because of both Doug's and my jobs. I do not think Logan even likes it."

"We can talk about that when you come over," Bill said. "You guys are practically family."

"We love you too."

"Hey Clare, how about we invite Lillian Shawn as well? I would not mind trying to make more sense out of all of this. I feel like the newbie in all of it."

"I think that is a great idea," Clarissa answered.

Bill hung up his phone, walked to the French doors, and opened them. The cold scent of the sea blasted him in the face. He breathed deeply and smiled.

The stone wall that enclosed the perimeter of the Shaw estate ran directly behind the manor, and there was less than ten feet between the building and the wall. When Bill had purchased the manor years ago, the wall had stood a mere four feet in height. Once Gaea was born, he and Cathy made the decision to make the area safer, not only for their child but for anyone who ventured near it. From the top of the wall to the rocks below was at least fifty feet and certain death for anyone that happened to fall.

Bill had chosen to have a decorative yet formidable iron fence attached to the top of the wall. It ran from the dense woods on the far southeastern corner to the far northeastern corner and effectively kept the wall safe from accidents. Not to be denied; young Aerin had challenged the wall and fence numerous times. He could stand on the wall but could not climb the fence, nor could he fit through the small openings between the pickets. After a few failed attempts, he gave up and began to explore the woods around the property.

Logan was not at the manor today, so Aerin was left to his own imagination. He put on his plastic army helmet and, grabbing his compass, decided to go exploring on the north side of the manor behind the garage.

It was a warm and sunny fall day, and as he made his way into the woods, sunlight was broken up by the tall trees casting shadows that danced across the bed of pine needles that he walked on. Aerin loved being within the realm of nature and breathed in the numerous smells. He began to jump from tree to tree, pretending to be an army soldier advancing on the enemy. He checked his compass, although he had no clue how to read it, and pretended to talk into a nonexistent radio. "Private Aerin, RECON specialist checking in." He spoke. "No sign of the enemy yet."

He looked for the next tree to run to, but all he could see were pine trees. He had brushed up against one of them once before and got a tongue lashing from Mrs. Douglas concerning the difficulties of cleaning pine tar from his clothing. Now he was resigned to jumping to the maple trees, and the closest one was thirty feet away. "Private Aerin again. Minefield ahead, but I am going to make a run for it." Taking a deep breath, he charged toward the maple tree. Within ten feet, he tripped on a root and went sprawling onto the ground, landing face up. Standing over him was a woman.

"Let's go over what we have." Dr. Tarpon said, tossing his napkin onto his plate. Brambilla held up a finger as he finished swallowing the last of his chocolate cake, pausing his colleague. He washed it down with a drink of red wine and wiped his mouth with his own napkin. "How can you eat chocolate cake and drink wine with it?" Jeffrey asked, making a sour face.

"I'm Italian," Roli said simply. "I just wish we had some espresso."

"American coffee served black will have to suffice."

Brambilla made his own face and poured a cup. "It seems that part of our hypothesis might be correct. Those ports would be open when the submarine dived."

"Right, but who is to say that the sub was not performing a routine dive, and something went wrong?" Tarpon asked, pouring himself a cup.

"If that were the case, then why is her hull intact?" Roli countered. "You said you have a theory."

"I do, but it might be difficult to prove."

"Go on." Brambilla said intrigued.

"Let us say that the captain did intend to scuttle his boat. It tends to reason that he would want to save his crew and could have cast them adrift prior to doing so."

"That is reasonable. Orders were not to have the boat captured but not the crew." Roli said.

"As far as we know, yes. A commander's crew was dear, and I don't think this captain would sacrifice them unnecessarily. He would count on the following enemy destroyer to rescue them."

"Agreed."

"So how would the captain and his officers sink the boat and flood all of it, not just the ballasts, to ensure it would not be recovered?" Tarpon asked.

"There is only one way," Roli said, deep in thought. "The main hatches. They would dive the boat with all the main hatches open."

"Exactly!" Tarpon exclaimed.

"We have not seen evidence of any of those being open." Brambilla countered.

"They might be but when the boat settled on the bottom, they might have swung closed and would seem to our cameras that they had not been opened. There are only three of them."

"Then we need to dive and use the arm on Portunus to test them. That would be the proof we need." Brambilla said smiling. "And the Aquabot is small enough it might be able it fit inside."

"Risk the mini-sub?"

"It might be worth the try."

"Tomorrow morning, then, my friend," Jeffrey said, holding up his cup.

"Tomorrow," Brambilla said and answered his toast.

"Daddy! Daddy!" Aerin screamed, climbing up the grand staircase and charging past Mrs. Douglas.

"Young man!" she scolded.

Aerin rushed into his parents' bedroom and scrambled up the wrought iron staircase calling his father again. "Daddy!"

"I am here, Aerin. Come up!" The boy flew into his father's arms, his young body shaking.

"Is everything alright, Mr. Pender?" Mrs. Douglas called from the bottom of the stairs.

"Oh yes. I will handle this. No worries."

"Fine. Call if you need anything."

"I will," Bill answered as he held his son. "Now, what is the trouble?"

"I...I was playing in the woods behind the garage." Aerin said through sniffles. "And there was a woman."

Bill held the boy away from him and looked at his tear-stricken face. "What woman?"

"I was running through the woods. I tripped and when I looked up, she was standing over me. She looked scary, Daddy."

"What did she look like?" Bill demanded.

"I only saw her face for a second, but she was wearing a long blue dress and had long light hair. She also had weird boots. Like the boots the soldiers wear in the movies. But they were taller in the back."

"Did you see the woman's eyes?" Bill asked.

"I'm not sure. I saw her face for a second before she walked away, leaving me on the ground."

"It is important, Aerin. Did you see her eyes?"

"The boy thought for a moment before answering.

"They were green."

"Are you absolutely sure?" Aerin nodded and started to cry again. Bill pulled his son to himself and hugged him fiercely, rocking him in his arms.

"What?" Cathy asked Bill.

"Aerin saw Lily today." He replied softly. The couple were lying in bed getting ready to sleep when Bill decided to bring up their son's experience in the woods.

"What was Lillian doing walking in our woods?" Cathy asked.

"Not Lillian Shawn, honey. He met Lily Shaw." Cathy sat straight up in bed and stared at her husband.

CHAPTER 12
The Visit

Gaea sat in her brother's room, talking to Aerin about what he had seen. The boy was still upset but he knew the one to talk to would be his sister. He didn't understand why, but he *felt* that she could explain things like this better than his mother could. "Most people would not have seen her." Gaea continued.

"But you would have, right?"

"Probably." She admitted. "I'm not sure. I haven't seen Lily Shaw in my life."

"I know it was her. It's the same woman that is in the paintings with that sea fishing guy." He said.

Gaea smiled. "Yes, Captain Shaw, Lily's husband."

"Aren't they dead?" Aerin asked timidly.

"They both died a very long time ago."

"Then why is she walking around my woods scaring me?" He asked angrily. "What is she, some sort of zombie come back from the grave?"

"Did she talk to you?" She asked.

"I don't think so, but I ran away so fast," Aerin said, picking up his GI Joe doll and fiddling with it. "She was a ghost, wasn't she?"

"I think so. We have a gift," Gaea explained, "and can see and even talk to dead people. I'm not sure how strong you are at this, and we probably won't know until you get older."

"So, you will help me?"

"Of course I will. You're my brother, and I love you, " she said, hugging Aerin.

Bill placed the items he had bought at the grocery store onto the counter. "Did they have everything on the list, Dad?" Vicky asked, unpacking a plastic bag.

"You bet, oh, except I had to substitute the live lobster with imitation crab."

"Then what is in that bag?" She asked, pointing at the only paper bag on the table and reaching for it.

Bill pulled it away from her and held it up in the air. "Artichokes. Extremely sensitive artichokes." He laughed.

"Give them to me before you hurt them!" Vicky shrieked.

He handed the lobster over, laughing harder. "Hurt them! And that boiling water bath you are going to put them into is a day at the spa?" Bill was laughing so hard tears were forming in his eyes.

Cathy walked into the kitchen. "And what is this ruckus?" She demanded.

"Dad's being a jerk," Vicky said, placing the bag on the counter and setting a large pot of water on high to boil.

"He's always being a jerk. So, what's new?"

"Wait." Bill pleaded. "How come I am always the jerk?"

"He's a natural at it," Cathy whispered to her daughter and they both broke out in laughter.

"Fine. I'm going up to Dreamer's Hideaway and write."

"Have fun." His wife called after him as he stomped up the back stairs.

"I love when you cook for our family." Cathy said opening the bag. "Nice ones but why only four of them? You are cooking for nine people."

"It's all I need for lobster bisque. It's going to be the soup starter along with the Caesar salad." Vicky explained.

"Yum. Can I help?"

"Sure. You can be my sous chef."

"What do I do?" Cathy asked.

"Open that bottle of wine, please. And no, it is not for drinking."

Cathy rolled her eyes.

Bill made his way down the hallway and paused at the partially opened door of his son's room. Inside, he could hear Gaea and Aerin talking about what had happened in the woods. He considered listening but then moved on. If there was anything he needed to know, he had confidence that his daughter would come to him. He continued toward his own bedroom and the widow's watch.

Mrs. Douglas had the day off, leaving her two subordinates to do the day's cleaning and prepare the dining room for the evening meal and the guests. Chrystal Wellwood and Karen Durham were working together, preparing the dining room and talking quietly. "I tell you, Karen, this house is haunted. Can't you hear the things at night?"

"It's an incredibly old manor. It is bound to have creaks and such." Karen replied. "But I admit I have heard some rather odd things."

Chrystal polished a piece of silverware and placed it next to a plate. "And Aerin. I've been overhearing some saying that he saw something in the attic when Mrs. Douglas caught him. Why the little brat was even up here in our personal quarters is beyond me."

"I don't think the child went into our rooms. Nothing was amiss in mine." Karen said, folding a napkin and placing it into a wine glass.

"Not in mine either. I love how you make things with napkins. That looks like a swan. Teach me someday?"

"Of course. It's easy. It was a requirement when I worked at the banquet hall back in London."

"You worked in England?" Chrystal asked.

"London, Ontario, up in Canada. Close to Toronto."

"I see. I didn't know you were Canadian."

"I'm not. Born and raised in Portland. I went to school up there for a time. Working in the hall helped to make ends meet. I never graduated."

"That's too bad. I've always wanted to go to college. Be a nurse, ya know?" Chrystal said.

"Do it. You are the only one that can make it happen." Karen remarked, adjusting a chair. "I think that this dining room is ready for guests."

"Me too. I'll get Mrs. Pender."

"And Chrystal, you can become a nurse if you put your mind to it."

"Thanks."

Doug and Clarissa showed up early as usual, and Logan and Aerin immediately charged out the door to play in the yard, followed closely by Piddles. Lick was scooped up by Cathy and brought back into the great room. "Naughty kitty." She said, placing him on the floor. Lick ran and hid under the piano. Cathy hugged her two guests. "Vicky has been hard at work preparing a masterpiece for us."

"Great!" Doug exclaimed. "I am starving. Where is Bill?"

"Where he normally is," Cathy replied, pointing upward. "He should be down shortly. I have found that when our daughter is cooking, all I have to do is open the windows in the kitchen and let the delectable aromas drift up. The one thing my husband can't resist is his stomach."

Clare laughed and handed Cathy a bottle of Pinot Grigio. "Mind if we raid the wine cellar?"

"Let's go do it," Cathy replied. "Maybe we can observe the master chef at work from the wet bar."

Bill had called Bob Pepper, not because he doubted his agent but simply because he wanted to hear the news from the horse's mouth.

"It's true, Bill. I'm done with the business. It's time to enjoy what's left of my life."

"It's just hard to believe," Bill said, pacing his office.

"I'm in my seventies, Bill. With this fire and all, I just realized it was too much. I want time with Dottie and your kids, for Christ's sake. They are the only kids I consider my grandchildren. I never had kids of my own."

"I know Bob, and they love you and Dorothy."

"I almost missed that fabulous meal that Vicky cooked for us because of the publishing house. Enough is enough. I appointed a new CEO for the time being until the merger takes place. After that, I don't care. I might even sell my stock in the company. Bill, I really don't want anything to do with it anymore."

"I guess I can understand that, especially wanting the kids around. As a father, I want them close, and when they are not, it makes my heart ache."

"Well, I guess I have to thank you for loaning yours to us."

"It's not my choice, Bob. They want to see you and Dottie. Especially Vicky. She is downstairs right now cooking for the family as well as Clare, Doug, their kid, and another guest that is coming soon."

"Lucky bastard. You know, if you don't fund a restaurant for that girl, I will."

"Perhaps we can do a joint venture. She still needs to go to and graduate from culinary school."

"She had damn well better choose a few business courses. Running a restaurant is not only cooking." Bob said gruffly.

"She plans on it, and I think she also has the best tutor she could ask for if she asks you for help."

Bill could not see him do it. Bob Pepper wiped tears from his eyes. "I have to go, Bill."

"Me too. I think dinner is about to be served. Talk soon, and we want you and Dottie to visit."

"You got it," Bob responded, and then the two men ended their phone call.

Bill sighed, closed the doors to the widow's watch, and headed downstairs. The aroma from the kitchen was too enticing. As Bill entered the great room, he was met with the sight of all his adult guests, including Gaea, sitting around the fireplace, engaged in conversation. All but Lillian, who stood in front of it, looking up at the painting of Wilbur and Lily that hung over the hearth.

"Quite the resemblance isn't there," Bill said, walking up to his guest.

"I looked like her fifteen years ago. It's remarkable, but Mr. Pender, she is my great-grandaunt. Anyway, she is long dead, is she not?"

"Perhaps," Bill said. "Questions have arisen about one Lily Shaw..." Lillian looked at him questioningly. Bill was saved by Clarissa, who had arrived to speak to Lillian. He excused himself and turned away to greet his other guests.

Vicky was finalizing her dishes with the help of Karen who had volunteered to stay and help serve the meal. She and Chrystal had been given the afternoon off, but Karen had opted to help, and Vicky was grateful. The amount of food she had cooked was more than ample for a party of nine and she was constantly reminding herself to adjust the portions as she cooked. Vicky had the timing down to near perfection. The amounts were just not acceptable. Too much was going to go to waste. "Vicky, you made so much," Karen said, ladling the lobster bisque into individual bowls.

Nearly all the cutlery, dishes, and serving utensils were original to the manor and had been painstakingly restored. The set was massive and could serve thirty people. Cathy had had the China cabinets that lined a wall of the dining room and the glass doors of each rebuilt. They had become a showcase of antiques. The addition of interior lighting to the cabinetry, along with glass shelves, enhanced the beauty and made the Shaw Manor dining room a spectacular place to enjoy a meal. The fine art that Cathy had brought home was incredible as well. All the serveware, dinnerware, silverware, and drinkware were Grand Baroque. All of which were used for dining quite frequently.

"I know," Vicky said, pulling out a tray of stuffed mushrooms from the oven.

"Mushrooms?" Karen asked.

"I had leftover lobster meat and needed something to do with it." She said, reaching for the fresh lemon juice she had squeezed.

"You are amazing."

"Hey, go change and join us," Vicky said.

"Vicky, that is not my place. You must remember I am just a servant in this house." Karen responded.

"Well, not to me. But OK. I get it. How about you, me, and Chrystal have some leftovers for lunch tomorrow?"

"Now, that would be appropriate," Karen said, smiling.

"We better call our guests into the dining room and start serving."

CHAPTER 13
Dinner & Delays

Madeline Johansson sat in the Smithsonian Research Library, pouring through microfilm. The young Swedish intern had no luck with the books she had gone through, and if the microfilm didn't produce anything, she would resort to the internet. She liked the old-school approach when it came to research, as the internet had proven to be unreliable in the past. At best, she considered it a place to get leads, not necessarily concrete results.

Johansson had found a metric ton of information on Anubis as well as hundreds of photos of the Egyptian God. All the images resembled one another. None of them came close to the pictures Mathew had taken of their statue. She was finding discrepancy after discrepancy between the two. The ears were much too short, and the paint scheme seemed wrong and did not conform to how the ancient Egyptians decorated their deities. The statue in the lab had fangs and the accepted versions of Anubis did not.

She made notes of everything that she found. As she had come to find out, Professor Ian McCloud demanded thoroughness, and Madeline was determined to deliver just that. She finished up with the last of the microfilm with disappointing results finding not so much as a clue of the statue's origin. It was time to explore the internet.

Tarpon and Brambilla were back on the bridge of the Scion of the Seas, staring at the monitors as the Portunus approached the foredeck hatch of U-116. Silt still floated through the lights of the mini-sub, somewhat obscuring its cameras. "It looks closed tight." Roland Brambilla noted.

"Perhaps. We need to get the claw of the Portunus onto it and try and lift it. If it was left un-battened, then it should swing open."

"If it is not rusted shut."

It took the remote pilot nearly an hour to maneuver the Portunus into the correct position to employ its robotic arm. There was no wheel on the outer side of the hatch as it was secured from within the pressure hull. The only thing to attempt to grab onto was a small maintenance handle that was partially obscured by the hatch. "Dammit all." The technician mumbled as he tried once again to grasp a handle that was meant to fit a man's hand. The claw of the robotic arm was larger. Another hour passed, and the technician sat back and threw up his arms in defeat. "The claw is just too large to grab it. I'm sorry, doctors."

"Let's move on and examine the conning tower and aft hatch. Maybe we will have better luck." Tarpon suggested.

"Agreed, let's move on," Brambilla said.

The pilot took the controls in hand, and the Portunus glided toward the next target. The remainder of the dive seemed to go the same as the first attempt. Both the conning tower hatch as well as the aft escape hatch appeared to be closed and the Portunus could not get ahold of the small handles. "That's it for the day," Tarpon stated. "Bring it back to the surface."

"Is there a smaller attachment for that robotic arm?" Brambilla asked Dr. Laurent.

"There is." She answered. "But it is back at MIT. It was being engineered and manufactured when we decided to join your expedition. A last-minute addition to the Portunus arsenal of features.”

“If it's ready, can it be flown out here?”

“You bet it can. I will call right now.”

“Damn delays,” Tarpon said. “I need some coffee.”

An hour later, Laurent delivered the news. “It's ready and being packed. We will have it here in three days.”

“Three days,” Tarpon said, rubbing his forehead. “It is what it is. What can we do in the meantime?”

“What if it's not what we think, Jeffrey? I think we should go back down and really look at the hull of the U-116.” Brambilla said. “Maybe we have missed something.”

Tarpon shook his head in doubt but agreed with the current assessment of the situation. “Can we cover all of the grids we lay out in that amount of time?”

“We can sure the hell try.” Dr. Laurent added.

“OK then. Roli and I will lay out the search grid. Please get the Portunus ready to dive.”

“We are going to need Aquabot as well,” Brambilla said.

“You are right, Roli.”

“I'll call over to the Archaean Horizon and have them prep the minisub.” Laurent acknowledged, then turned and left.

“This might be a red herring Roli, but it will give us a complete video and photographic record of the wreck. This was in our plans to do in any case.”

"True. Who knows, we just might turn up something unexpected."

"We usually do, Roli. We usually do." Tarpon agreed.

"Sit down, Vicky. I can manage this." Karen whispered.

"My guests. I'm helping." She responded. "Besides, I have to plate all of this food."

Karen rolled her eyes and carried the tray of piping hot soup into the dining room. Carefully she began to ladle it into the bowls before the guests. "What do we have here?" Lillian asked.

"Lobster bisque," Karen replied. "And Vicky baked the crusty sourdough bread this morning." She added, nodding to the baskets on the table.

"Yum!" Doug said, pulling the white napkin off from the nearest basket and taking a piece of the warm bread.

"What are they saying?" Vicky asked when Karen returned to the kitchen.

"Not much. They are all too busy stuffing their faces."

Vicky giggled.

"What is next?"

"The shrimp Caesar salad with freshly crushed anchovies and the lobster stuffed baby Bella mushrooms. Just keep an eye…"

"I know. Watch and wait for the last person to finish before serving the next course." Karen interrupted. "I can remove the bowls as they finish them."

Vicky smiled. "I keep forgetting your experience in the formal restaurant industry. I'm sorry."

"Don't be. Let's get the next tray ready to take over."

"Bill, I am stealing Vicky," Clarissa said, sopping up the remains of her soup with the bread. "Where in the world did she learn to cook like this?"

"Dorothy Pepper started it years ago. The rest is self-taught. She is planning on going to culinary school next year." Cathy said, wiping her mouth with her napkin.

Bill began to pass a wine bottle around the table. "We are very lucky."

Karen picked up the last bowl and left for the kitchen. The guests quickly worked through the salad and the mushrooms and started to dig into the main course of fried haddock with the option of pork tender loin. The chef stood at the doorway of the dining room, still dressed in her smock, watching her happy guests.

"Vicky, this is amazing," Doug said, watching Karen remove the cloche from both platters.

"I agree. What a splendid take on 'surf and turf.' And the fresh greens look delicious!" Lillian exclaimed.

"What is the ingredient in your mashed potatoes? I can't quite place it," Clare asked, tasting the potatoes.

"Freshly ground nutmeg," Vicky replied.

"Nutmeg in potatoes. Simply brilliant." Clare replied.

"I need to prep the dessert," Vicky said and left.

"Dessert?" Doug asked, rubbing his stomach. "I am stuffed as it is."

Karen smiled as she took his plate. "I think you will find the room, sir." Before bringing out the dessert, Karen placed small wine glasses in front of the guests.

"What are these? Goblets for small people?" Bill asked.

Vicky appeared carrying two bottles and placed them in front of her father. Both looked like half-sized bottles of wine. "Can you do the honors, Dad?"

Bill picked up one of the bottles and found it very cold. He turned it and read the label aloud. "*Eiswein*. Vicky, where did you get this?" He asked.

"A gift from Grandpa. He thought it would go well with my dessert."

"You bet it will."

"Honey, what is it?" Cathy asked.

"Allow me," Doug broke in. Eiswein, as it is called in German, is a dessert wine made from frozen grapes that are still on the vine when harvested. It is quite delicious and sweet." As Doug finished speaking, Karen began to place the desserts on the table.

"No way," Clare stated. "Is this what I think it is?"

"It is Baked Alaska, which happens to be one of my favorites," Lillian said.

Twenty minutes later, Vicky reappeared as the espresso was being served. "I hope everyone found the food satisfactory." She spoke.

"What? It was beyond that young lady. I'm going to sleep for a month." Doug exclaimed.

"Honey, it was spectacular," Lillian said. Everyone agreed.

"You did it again, sis," Gaea said, standing up and going over to hug her sister. "Aren't you going to eat?"

"I have lots of leftovers. Karen and I will have some in the kitchen. I'll give some to Crystal and Mrs. Douglas tomorrow if they want it."

"It really was amazing."

"Can we go up to my room, Mom?" Aerin asked. The boys had been remarkably quiet all through the meal and now seemed tired and ready to get away.

"Of course, you can," Cathy said.

"Logan, you want to sleep over?" Clare asked.

"Yes!"

"Okay with you, Cat?"

"Absolutely," Cathy answered as the two slid off their chairs and scrambled out of the dining room.

An hour later, everyone but Vicky and Karen had retired to the great room and were sitting around the fireplace. Bill had offered after-dinner drinks, and all declined except for Doug. He sat with a small glass of port in front of him. "Cleans my palate after drinking that heavy coffee, " he had explained.

"Well, let's get down to why we are all here," Clare said, adjusting herself on the sofa. "How are you doing, Gaea?"

"I'm OK." She answered. "I have been using the charismatic shield that Lillian showed me. It seems to work."

Lillian sighed in relief. "I had been worried that I had failed."

"Do you sense anything in the manor right now?" Doug asked.

"Nothing," Gaea spoke. He looked at Lillian, who shook her head.

"We will leave the attic to another time," Cathy said. "We have another issue."

"Oh, and that is?" Lillian asked.

"My son saw something in the woods, and it scared the hell out of him."

"He is a medium as well," Gaea added. "Or at least I believe him to be."

"What did he see?" Lillian asked.

"Not what, but who," Bill said, standing and then pouring himself a glass of ice water.

"Lily Shaw," Gaea stated simply.

It was Lillian's turn to stand. She walked and looked up at the painting once again. "She has never been seen at the manor after her death by the living?"

"Not that we know of," Cathy replied.

"That is troubling, then. We have a sighting of her daughter Rebecca, and now her mother is wandering the estate."

"What do you think it means?" Gaea asked.

Lillian turned and looked at the girl. "What would you be doing if you were a mother and your daughter was missing?"

"Or in trouble," Doug said softly.

"Perhaps a visit up to the attic sooner than later is in order after all. Gaea will accompany me when we go…"

"Now, wait a minute." Bill broke in, alarmed.

"There is no danger. Your daughter and I will simply go up and have a feel around, so to speak."

Cathy looked nervous.

"I will agree to it on one condition. Doug and I will be at the bottom of the stairs while you both are up there. Any sign of trouble and I'm coming to get my daughter." Bill demanded.

Lillian nodded her assent and turned back to the painting. "Great grandaunt, what are you doing?"

Lily Shaw stared back lifelessly with piercing green eyes.

CHAPTER 14
A Circus Act

It was an off remark by another intern that sent Madeline Johansson's research in a completely different direction. She had been having lunch in the cafeteria when she overheard two interns from another department talking about their plans for the weekend. It wasn't that one of them planned to go to see a rock concert, it was the other's plans to go to the circus over in Virginia. The thought of the various shows and acts that a circus put on got her thinking. Maybe the statue of Anubis was not created for an evil purpose. What if it was simply a prop? Madeline dropped her half-eaten sandwich into the trash bin and headed out the door.

The girl almost forgot to knock before she barged into Professor McCloud's office. Instead, she knocked and stood fidgeting outside of the closed door for a moment until she heard him say, come.

"Ah, Madeline. How goes the research?" He asked. "And please sit down."

"Dead end. But I have a new theory that I would like to explore with your permission."

"Go on."

"I have been pursuing the idea that our statue had been made with the occult in mind. You know, devil worship and such."

"That was the presumption, yes." McCloud agreed.

"Well, the discrepancies between the known depictions of Anubis, the Egyptian deity, and the one in the lab are almost to the point of being inane. The ears are too short, and it has fangs. Fangs Professor!"

"I have to admit it is somewhat silly."

"Professor, what if this statue was made to be nothing more than a prop for something? It might be one of a kind and extremely difficult to identify unless it has been captured somewhere in a photograph."

"You are proposing to find a picture of our statue somewhere in time that might have been randomly taken? Madeline that could take years."

"Give me a week."

McCloud stood up and paced back and forth behind his desk. "OK. You have your week. It will take that long for the carbon dating results to come back. I can't say I am not completely convinced that you are correct. It is worth looking into."

"Thank you, sir!" She exclaimed as she stood, and then left.

McCloud sat back down and sighed. He could not help but think that his intern was starting her own circus act.

Even Mrs. Douglas was impressed by the meal that Vicky had cooked for her family and guests as she ate happily with Karen and Chrystal in the kitchen. The older woman had advocated for a resident kitchen staff when she was first hired, however, it was proven unnecessary over time. The Penders rarely had large gatherings such as they had the previous night; thus, serving and cleanup were rarely required by her staff.

Karen had volunteered to stay and assist Vicky, and the two of them had cleaned up the aftermath. Mrs. Douglas was pleasantly surprised when she came back to the manor early in the morning to a spotless kitchen, and she did not let the fact go unnoticed or unmentioned. "You did an outstanding job last evening, Karen. I was not expecting to come back to such a clean kitchen, and the dining room looks like it was never used."

"Thank you, ma'am. I really like working with Vicky when she decides to cook."

"Well, this is certainly delicious," Chrystal commented. "Even warmed up."

"It is and I will commend her when I see her." Mrs. Douglas said with a smile.

Their lunch was interrupted by a loud crash coming from the dining room. They all ran toward the sound with Mrs. Douglas leading the way. Throwing open the door, they were met by the sight of one of the China cabinet glass doors shattered on the floor, yet nothing seemed amiss inside of it. All the dishes placed inside were unmoved and undamaged. "What in the blue blazes?" The head housekeeper said examining the cabinet. "Chrystal, get a broom and a dustpan. Karen, help me move these chairs out of the way." Both girls jumped into action.

Bill arrived a few moments later having heard the crash from his bedroom. "What the hell?" He demanded.

"We were having lunch in the kitchen when we heard the crash, Mr. Pender. No one was in there, and nothing inside the cabinet was damaged or even moved. The door just shattered for no apparent reason." Mrs. Douglas explained.

Bill took a moment to examine the door and scratched his head. "I don't get it."

"How do these things happen?" Karen asked.

Bill shook his head. "Well, I'll call Danny Hanson over in Limerick. He was the one who restored these in the first place. I know he can repair it."

"Very good, Mr. Pender." Mrs. Douglas spoke. "We will finish tidying up here."

Lillian Shawn sat on her veranda and looked out over the Marginal Way at the Atlantic. A cold breeze blowing in off the ocean caused her to draw a shawl over her shoulders. The hot tea she was sipping took away some of the frigid bite she was feeling.

She was also not feeling comfortable about her dinner with the Penders at Shaw Manor. Something didn't sit well with her. It wasn't that she had sensed anything during the visit. In fact, the house seemed to be quite peaceful. Still, she felt that something was not right in the home. Lillian just could not put her finger on it. The dozens of investigations she had done over the years told her as much.

She also knew that if there was something amiss the answer might reside in the attic, and she needed to get in there soon. She was concerned about what had been seen in the attic as well as the sighting of Lily Shaw wandering the estate. Gaea and her brother, both being mediums, intensified the worry she felt. Lillian had made some inquiries into this man, Jack Jefferson, through her friends, who were experts in the field of the paranormal. None of them had heard of him, except for one that knew him only as an up-and-coming writer. Or at least he had been.

Lillian did know of Jack's tragic death at Shaw Manor, although the reason seemed sketchy. Her delicate inquiries at the dinner party had produced little, if any, information, as the conversation was primarily about Gaea. The pieces of the puzzle that had been laid before her were not falling into place easily. Perhaps Lillian was going to have to make harder inquiries if she were to take on this investigation.

She was pleasantly surprised to see Gaea at her gate. Lillian buzzed her in and waited as the girl walked up the hill to greet her. "What a lovely surprise, Gaea!" the older woman said, hugging her.

"We need to talk," Gaea said flatly.

"Very well. Please sit down and have some tea. It is dreadfully cold this morning. How can I help?"

"I want to talk to you about Jack Jefferson."

It had taken less than forty-eight hours for Madeline Johansson to find the answer she was looking for. She had followed her own instincts and backed them up with science. She picked up the printouts and stuffed them into a file folder. She then headed for Professor McCloud's office.

Dr. Bastien hung up the phone and laughed. He dialed Cathy Pender. "A prop for a haunted house attraction?" Cathy said stunned. "I saw what that thing did here at my house doctor."

"Nevertheless, Professor Ian McCloud at the Smithsonian has confirmed it. The statue was created for The Egyptian Tombs of Horrors haunted attraction that used to operate just outside of Chicago. It ran for a few years then went out of business. The contents of the attraction were sold off or thrown out. Somehow, this statue found its way into your shop up here in Maine."

"How the hell did it get possessed?" Cathy asked half to herself.

"That is another question to be answered," Bastian said. "McCloud is sending it over to his parapsychology department. It seems he has a couple of psychic mediums on staff that are going to look at it. From a scientific and historical point of view, the case is closed. It is what you thought it was. A fake made for a single purpose, and it was not to deceive. It was to help scare the bejesus out of people."

"So, Jack was a medium as well?" Lillian asked taking a sip of tea.

"Yes," Gaea said simply. "He was a writer like my dad and had come to do book signings here in Maine. Bob Pepper, along with Clarissa, sent him up from New York. They thought that with my dad's aid, it would help him a lot."

"I see. So, what led you to believe that he was gifted?"

"My mom had brought a statue into the house, and I hated it the minute I saw it sitting next to the piano. It reeked of evil."

"And you think she did this on purpose?" Lillian asked.

"No!" Gaea answered adamantly. "My mom is not like you and me. She thought it was just a piece of art."

"I see. Do you want to talk about what happened that night?"

Gaea sighed and slumped back in her chair. "It was after me. Jack wouldn't let me go with him into the house. He tried to teach me the charismatic shield but there wasn't time. The demon was becoming stronger."

"Wait a moment," Lillian said setting down her cup. "Are you telling me that this was a demonic possession?"

"Yes. And somehow Jack knew the name of the demon. He knew a lot about it. I never knew why, and he died before I could ask him."

"Do you remember the name of the demon Gaea?"

The girl nodded and whispered a name. "Belphegor."

Lillian's jaw dropped and she whispered. "One of the princes of Hell."

"That is what Jack said."

"But the statue was destroyed."

Gaea shifted in her chair. "We thought so. Jack grabbed it and fell over the railing in the widow's watch onto the rocks. Dad said it shattered."

Lillian's mind was racing. She had no experience with anything demonic. Learning of such yes, but dealing with it? No. She had heard of the beast Belphegor, and it was starting to make sense. The demon was a defiler of souls, especially the young. From her studies, the demon was perhaps one of the worst in the realm of Hades. "If the statue was destroyed then the beast would have been released," Lillian stated.

"That is the problem. It wasn't destroyed. A fisherman found it. I have heard my mom and dad talking. I don't think they want me to know."

"What do you want to know?"

"Aerin has seen what appears to be Jack in our attic. I don't sense Jack's presence at all. Can a demon possess the dead?"

Aerin was playing in the front yard with Piddles when the dog began to bark. It ran toward the garage and stopped short. It looked back at the boy and then started to growl, facing the structure. Aerin ran to the dog and wrapped his arms around the Boxer's neck while hugging it. "What is it, Piddles? There is nothing there." Piddles whined and lay on the ground.

Aerin stood and walked slowly toward the woods at the west end of the garage. He thought he could see a figure standing just inside the edge of the trees. As he walked closer it seemed to recede deeper into the woods. He looked back and Piddles remained on the lawn panting. "C'mon Piddles. Come here." The dog refused and continued to whine.

The boy moved cautiously forward and found himself at the edge of the woods. He tried to peer through the dense foliage but could see nothing but shadows that were created by the sun filtering through the canopy. He turned and looked at Piddles and shrugged. The dog cocked its head. Aerin turned back toward the woods and was met by a woman in a long blue dress with blond hair. She leaned forward, her face inches from his, her green eyes penetrating the boys. "Save Rebecca." She whispered.

Aerin fell backward and started to crawl toward Piddles, who remained lying on the ground. He stood and began to run toward the manor, Piddles on his heels. Reaching the front porch, he looked back. The woman was nowhere to be seen.

CHAPTER 15
Come Out Wherever You Are

The second sighting of Lily Shaw did not go over well with Bill and Cathy Pender. For the time being, the woods surrounding the estate were restricted to pairs. To venture into them, Aerin would have to be with an adult or one of his sisters. His friend Logan would not suffice.

Gaea had gone to visit Lillian, and Vicky had headed off to the grocery store when the event occurred. Cathy had gone in to work in the store in Kennebunkport, and Bill was up in the widow's watch working on his novel. When Aerin came charging up to find his father, he was terrified. It took Bill nearly an hour to calm his son down enough to find out what had happened. Once he did, he was on the phone with his wife. "Babe, Aerin saw Lily Shaw again," He began, "and she spoke to him."

"Is this ever going to end?" Cathy replied, clearly upset. "What did she say?"

"Save Rebecca."

"Christ. Is he okay? Should I come home?"

"He's doing better. Unfortunately, Gaea is not home, and neither is Vicky. I think I will let him stay up in my office with me for a bit."

"Good idea. I should be there in a couple of hours." She said, sighing. "Bill, we have to do something."

"I'm going to give Clare a call and see if they can come over later. I think it is time we take a walk up to the attic."

"I have been dreading Gaea going up there."

"She will be with Lillian. It will be OK." Bill tried to say reassuringly.

"Are you going to call her as well?" Cathy asked.

"I thought I would let Gaea do that when she gets home. She is a big part of all of this and probably knows more about what is going on than we do. Thank God she is on our side."

"We just might need him as well," Cathy said.

"Who?"

"God."

A few hours later, the family was together at the manor. Vicky was putting her groceries away in the kitchen, and Gaea was on the phone with Lillian. Cathy was talking with her son in front of the fireplace as Looney Tunes played on the TV. Bill was in the dining room with Hanson Custom Cabinetry.

"I don't get it." Danny Hanson said, examining the cabinet door he had just removed. "The wood is cracked. It seems that the entire frame is warped which caused the glass to break. I have no clue as to what would cause this."

"Me neither. Can you fix it?" Bill lied. He had his suspicions about the cause, but the carpenter didn't need to know them.

"Of course. I'll have to partially rebuild it, but I can repair it. Give me a month?"

"Why so long?"

"It's not the woodwork, Mr. Pender. It's the glass. The glass on the rest of the cabinetry is over a hundred years old. I just can't put in a new piece and have it look correct. Look at the other door. See the waves in the glass?" Bill looked at it and nodded. "Over time, glass flows. Given enough time, say thousands of years, it will flow right out of its frame. I need to find another piece of glass to match this."

"I see," Bill said. Cathy would care more about this than he did. "Take all the time you need. We are in no hurry."

Bill walked the carpenter out and watched him load the cabinet door into his van. He closed the front door and walked back toward the kitchen. Cathy had finished talking with Aerin and was pouring herself a glass of wine. "He's still pretty shaken up, Bill."

"I would be too." He said, reaching into the mini-fridge for a beer.

Gaea wandered into the kitchen and plopped down on a stool at the island. "Hey, sis." Vicky said cheerfully.

"Hi."

"So?" Bill asked.

"So, Lillian will be here around eight. She can't come sooner."

"That will be good," Bill replied. "Clare told me that she has to wait for Doug to finish up at USM and they can be here around seven."

"I'm glad he got that job at the University of Southern Maine. He was getting sick of running to New York all the time." Cathy remarked.

"Dad, what about Aerin and Logan when Lillian and I... well, you know."

"They stay down here with Clarissa and Mom. Right honey?"

"I don't like it, but yes. And Vicky you will be down here with us as well."

"The hell I will!" She exclaimed angrily.

"Vicky!" Bill admonished.

The girl tossed a dishrag onto the counter and confronted her parents. "Look, I have a stake in this. Gaea is my sister. I will not be relegated to having to sit down here while she walks into potential danger. Do I have to remind you that I have been in the attic and was attacked in it? I will be at the bottom of the stairs with Dad and that is final!"

Bill looked at his wife wide-eyed. Cathy had no strength to argue and simply said, "Fine."

"Well, OK then," Bill said. "Bottom of the stairs with us. Fair Vicky?"

"Fair."

Dr. Tarpon stood on the weather deck of the Scion of the Seas just outside of the ship's bridge. The sky was overcast, and a frigid wind hit him in the face. It felt like the season was changing, and the time limit left to examine the U-116 wreck was closing quickly. The helicopter from the Archaean Horizon had left before dawn for Halifax, Nova Scotia, where it was to pick up the new equipment for the Portunus, and the detailed mapping of the hull of the wreck was only 75% complete. Jeffrey Tarpon had never felt so pressed for time during his lengthy career as a marine archeologist.

"Do you need to go over to the Horizon for any reason?" Captain Hilton asked, joining him.

"Not at the moment, " he replied, pulling the collar of his coat further up around his neck. Below him, he could see the skiff being loaded. "Why?"

"Suspension of operations, I am afraid. There is a storm moving in from the north, and things are going to get nasty. I've ordered the removal of the floating docks and the skiff to be pulled by the Horizon. The MIT team is also suspending operations."

"Dammit." He said softly.

She patted the scientist gently on the back. "We may have to leave the site temporarily so that we can turn into the storm. The dynamic positioning system probably can't hold us in place, and it might be dangerous to try."

"What about the helicopter?" He asked.

"It should be here shortly and well in advance of the storm. Captain DeWight is preparing for its arrival now. If we have time, the skiff will run the parts over before we need to lift the boat onto the Horizon's deck."

Dr. Brambilla stepped out onto the weather deck carrying a backpack. He hugged Tarpon for a moment. "I have to get back to the Archaean Horizon, Jeffrey."

Jeff nodded and watched his friend climb down the stairs that led to the floating dock and climb aboard the boat. Every time Roli left him Jeffrey could feel the sadness that filled the other man. Being a scientist, Tarpon had little time for such empathy, but he had no control over these feelings, so he did his best to try to ignore them with little luck. He watched as the skiff cast off and headed toward the sister research ship. Captain Patricia Hilton had returned to the bridge, leaving Tarpon alone.

Professor McCloud had just received the preliminary report from the team of mediums. In all, four people had been studying the statue over the last few days. The team leader stood in his office with the written report in her hands, and she looked concerned. "What have you found?" the professor asked the younger dark-haired woman. Long ago, he might have found her rather attractive.

"Troubling information Professor. Everything seems residual but recent. I do not mean a hundred years recent. A decade or so, and there was a violent death associated with this item."

"Oh?"

She laid the file before him on his desk and stood back. He opened it and took some time to read the two-page summary before sitting back. "Demonic possession of an inanimate object?" He asked.

"It is not unheard of, sir. I can cite examples dating back to…"

The professor raised his hand, silencing her. "No need, Darleen. I can grasp this. I have a degree also. More than one."

"Of course, Professor."

"Do you know the name of this potential demon?"

"No. The residual information that we could glean was not strong enough to be conclusive."

"I will read your entire findings, Darleen. Your suggestions on what to do with the statue?"

"Except to someone that collects old amusement items, it's junk."

"If you are done with it, tag it and send it over to our storage area for now."

"You got it, Professor."

The arrival of Lillian was heralded by Piddle's excessive barking at the front door. Upon opening it, Cathy was met not only by the medium but also by a man of the cloth. "This is Father Dickinson," Lillian said, introducing the man. "He is here as a friend and not as a representative of the church." She said, stepping into the great room.

"Not representing the church?" Cathy questioned.

"He is not an exorcist," Lillian replied. "He is simply here to help me and anyone else with emotional support."

"I see," Cathy said. "Please come in."

An hour later, Cathy, Clarissa, the boys, and the priest were gathered in the great room. Gaea and Lillian were ready to go into the attic. Vicky and Doug stood by as Bill unlocked the door. Flipping the light switch, the yellowish bulb turned on at the top of the stairs and illuminated a portion of the attic in an eerie glow. "I can't believe you never had proper lighting installed up there," Doug said.

"I never got around to it," Bill said, moving aside for Lillian and Gaea to pass. "Any trouble, you scream. Got it?"

Vicky reached out and hugged her sister. "Please be careful."

"We will," Gaea replied, hugging her back.

"Close the door behind us, please," Lillian asked. Bill nodded.

Lillian took Gaea's hand as they made their way up the narrow stairwell. At the top of the stairs, Lillian was met by the sight of a mannequin and a few crates with no tops. Everything inside appeared to be junk. She held her finger to her lips as she looked at Gaea. The attic was quiet as both women closed their eyes and began their mental exploration of the space. Neither of them could detect anything until they heard a shuffling at one end of the long attic.

"Pain," Lillian whispered.

"Fear," Gaea mumbled.

Bill locked the attic door with Doug's help as the three women made their way down the grand staircase. Vicky was noticeably concerned as they made their way to the fireplace and sat down. "You OK, sis?" She asked.

"Yeah, I think so. We didn't see anything, but I felt a lot of emotion. Did you, Lillian?"

"I felt pain and fear, but I couldn't discern who it was coming from."

"Tracy is very afraid for Rebecca. Both were up there but hiding." Gaea said softly.

"Hiding from what?" Bill asked, taking a seat and joining the group.

"I would like to know that myself." Doug echoed, heading for the bar.

They were all surprised by Aerin speaking up. "The Devil. He is hiding as well, and the ghosts are afraid of him."

"Honey, the Devil?" Cathy asked, moving to the floor next to her son.

"I hear him in my head. He says he is a prince, and I should go with him." Aerin spoke to his mother.

"Bill…" Cathy said, looking up at her husband.

CHAPTER 16
Nightmares

For the next week, Shaw Manor remained quiet, and a sense of normalcy replaced the chaos that seemed to threaten to break out. It took all Bill Pender had to keep his wife from taking the children and leaving the house. Father Dickinson had promised to elevate their situation in the church but could not promise anything. He was simply a man of the cloth who was authorized to perform basic church functions at the lowest level of the diocese hierarchy.

Vicky and Gaea had chosen to take another weekend to visit the Peppers and took Aerin with them. The break was welcomed by both Bill and Cathy, who in turn chose to get away themselves, booking a romantic suite at the Mount Washington Hotel in New Hampshire. Cathy loved the fall in New England. The leaves were turning lavish colors, and the peak of Mt. Washington itself was already covered in snow. She had always been torn between her love of the mountains and the ocean. With her kids safely up with Bob and Dottie Pepper, she was finally able to relax to a certain extent. Knowing there were still problems at home, I nagged at her. A good night's sleep and a hot shower helped greatly.

Bill had gotten up earlier and went to explore the hotel's spectacular lobby. He stopped at the concierge and made a reservation for breakfast at a special table with a view of Mt. Washington. He also started planning his and his wife's day.

Cathy dressed and went into the bathroom to check her hair and brush her teeth. The suite that Bill had rented was large and elegant, with a fireplace in the sitting area. The bathroom was equally beautiful. She washed her face and looked up. A woman wearing a white dress with black hair was standing behind her. She shrieked and spun around, coming face to face with Bill. "You scared the hell out of me," Cathy said, scolding her husband.

"I'm sorry, babe. We have reservations downstairs for breakfast..." He said apologetically.

"Do not sneak up on me. It has been a tough couple of days."

Bill pulled her to him and embraced her. "I shut the door quite loudly and called your name."

"I didn't hear you." She sighed.

"C'mon." Bill broke the embrace. "I'm starving."

Gaea had taken her brother into downtown Bar Harbor to do some shopping, however it was a ruse. She wanted some alone time with Aerin to talk to him about what he thought was in the Shaw Manor's attic. They spent a couple of hours in the shops, and both bought some new clothes for school as well as notebooks, pens, and pencils. She had to admit that her brother had somewhat of an eclectic taste when it came to his clothing. His choice of a pair of purple jeans and a yellow pullover seemed strange, and Gaea wasn't sure if her mother would approve. She shrugged it off. He was wearing it, not her.

The two ended up at an ice cream shop that was still open even though most of the shops had or were closing for the season. Aerin had no problem digging into the cone of Rocky Road even though the weather was not good. There was light rain, and the wind coming off the ocean was bitter. Gaea shook her head, bundled up, and sipped her latte. "Aerin, tell me about the voice that talks to you. The one in your head."

He shrugged and looked at his sister. "It talks to me at night, mostly when I'm asleep. Sometimes it's really scary." He said, eating another bite.

"I can imagine. I don't like nightmares, either. Do Tracy and Rebecca talk to you?"

"Sometimes."

"Why only sometimes?" She asked. "Do you know?"

"When the devil is not there, then they are not afraid and will."

"What do they say to you?"

"That they want help to run away," Aerin stated flatly. "Rebecca wants her mom but even she is afraid to come help."

Gaea took a deep breath as she took in and tried to process what her brother was telling her. She had sensed and knew about Tracy and Rebecca because she felt their presence. Lily was new, and her brother had seen her twice. Her ghost had spoken to Aerin the second time and scared the crap out of him.

"Has this devil told you his name?" Gaea asked.

"He calls himself a prince and wants me to come join him, " he said, finishing off the remainder of this waffle cone. Shaking, he bundled up. Gaea motioned for the waitress and ordered a hot chocolate, which she brought quickly after taking a look at the shivering boy. He grabbed the cup and blew on it before taking a sip. "He told me his name was Bal...Bal...I'm sorry, I can't remember."

"Listen to me," Gaea said, leaning forward, "Did he say his name was Belphegor?"

Aerin nodded.

The couple had eaten at the Rosebrook within the Mt. Washington Hotel before. But it was a long time ago. They had talked of taking their honeymoon at the storied hotel, but it never came to fruition. A quick, non-descript wedding led them both to the renovation of the Shaw Manor and then back to work. Deadlines controlled their lives. Then, Gaea entered the picture. Thoughts of a proper honeymoon gave way to diapers and raising their daughter. With the addition of Vicky, and then Aerin, the couple had settled into the routine of raising a normal American family. As normal as possible.

Bill set his car keys, the room key, and a brochure on the table before pulling out a chair for his wife. After they were both seated, a waiter arrived, placed menus in front of the couple, and left with the promise of coffee. "What is this?" Cathy asked, picking up the brochure.

"Today's activity," Bill said, smiling.

"The Mt. Washington Cog train?" She read aloud. "It will be freezing up there. Look at that mountain." She exclaimed, pointing to the snow-capped peak in the distance.

"I packed our winter coats."

Cathy covered her mouth with her hand and laughed. "You are full of surprises, aren't you?"

The waiter returned and filled their cups with piping hot coffee. "Have you decided?" He asked.

"Not yet," Bill answered.

"Oh, I see you are staying in Princess Catheryn's room. Have you seen her?" The waiter asked.

"I don't know what you're talking about," Bill replied.

"I see you have not taken the hotel tour. She is the resident ghost here at the hotel. The wife of the man who built Mt. Washington. Rooms three and fourteen were her rooms of choice. Have you seen her?"

"Not me," Bill said. "I slept like a baby last night."

Cathy's face turned white.

Upon returning to Pepper Mansion, Gaea was beside herself with what to do. Aerin had confirmed that the demon was still back home at Shaw Manor and that Tracy and Rebecca, although ghosts, were trapped in the attic and terrified. Lily was wandering the estate grounds, and she seemed afraid to enter the manor to help her own distraught child.

Vicky was in the kitchen with Dottie making cookies. Aerin was in the den with Bob listening to the old man talk about the model trains that adorned shelving attached to the walls. Gaea was struggling with whom to call with what she had learned. Clarissa would no doubt call her parents and there was no way she was calling them with this kind of news. Not yet. The only option was to call her new mentor Lillian Shawn.

Lillian had been reading a book in her dining room when Gaea called. "Lillian Shawn." She answered cheerfully.

"Hi, Lillian, this is Gaea, and I think we have a bigger problem than we thought."

"Tell me."

Forty-five minutes later the older medium was convinced that the Penders were once again plagued with a demon in their home. The question that Gaea had posed on their first meeting haunted her as she had found no answer to the question. Could a demon possess the dead? Lillian had her own guesses but nothing substantial to tell the girl. Others in her own circles had opinions and nothing more. Her guess was a possibility but was weak at best. She surmised that when Jack had given his life to destroy the statue, the demon had invaded Jack when he was still alive. Once dead, perhaps Belphegor clung to the boy's soul in death, refusing to release it to the light. It had attached itself to an inanimate object, so why not the soul of a dead person?

Lillian shook her head in confusion. She had no formal training in demonology, and her only experience was just unfolding. Ignoring Gaea's wishes, she called Clarissa. Perhaps there was news from Father Dickinson. One thing she was convinced of was that when dealing with a demon, a qualified and ordained exorcist was needed.

Bill received a call from Clarissa as he and Cathy were boarding the cog train. By the time she had explained the issues conveyed by his daughter through Lillian and what she had to say, the train was halfway to the summit of the mountain. He was careful with his replies to Clare as his wife was listening, keeping them short and terse. He saw no reason to alarm his wife and telling her of these things could wait. Upon hanging up, Bill simply told Cathy that it was his agent calling about work. He sat back and looked at his wife as she gazed out the window at the brilliant foliage that autumn in New Hampshire created. At least for the next few hours, she could enjoy some peace. Bill Pender, however, could not.

Robert Pepper knew how to read people, and simply looking at Gaea, he knew something was not right. The boy was a paradox to him, seeming to let most things slide off from him like a sheet of snow off a roof. His sister was different. He could see the concern in her eyes for Aerin, and the girl was nervous. He could not guess why, but he was determined to find out. When an appropriate time availed itself, he asked Gaea to join him in this office.

"Talk to me," Pepper said, sitting at his desk and looking at the young woman across from him. "What is bothering you?"

"Nothing," Gaea said.

"You cannot lie to me, young lady. I have been doing this way too long. I can see trouble all over your face."

Gaea sat back and looked toward the bank of windows and out at the Atlantic Ocean. She crossed her arms and sighed. "It's back." She said simply.

"What is back?" Pepper demanded.

"You don't have to get angry with me!" Gaea shouted at the older man. "I'm not one of your employees."

"Of course, you are not," Bob said softly. "It's just an awfully bad habit I can't rid myself of. I am sorry. I just care deeply about you as well as your brother and sister. Please let me help."

"I am not sure you can. The thing at the manor has come back."

He patiently listened to Gaea explain for a time. Bob knew the story of what had happened that caused Jack's death and, quite frankly, was happy he had not been there to witness it. "I never knew its name," Pepper said, standing and walking to the window. "I guess I never wanted to. What else did Aerin tell you?"

"The demon wants him. Belphegor wants to take him away. Grandpa, I'm afraid for my brother." Gaea began to cry.

Robert himself could feel tears welling up in his own eyes but held them back. He was a strong man, but he still had empathy, especially for those that he loved. Turning, he walked to Gaea and sat on the corner of his desk, looking down at the girl. He took a handkerchief from his pocket and handed it to her. She took it and wiped her eyes. "Lillian said she would help but she is not as strong as Jack was. I am not strong enough either, and Aerin is too young. I feel like we are living in never-ending nightmares. I know that I am."

"Honey, I can help."

"How?"

Robert Pepper stood and walked around his desk before taking a seat. Smiling, he picked up his phone and dialed a number. He put his finger to his lips, shushing Gaea, and waited for an answer.

Father Dickinson was sitting in his superior's office listening to the elder man rake him over the coals for a third time.

"Father, there is simply not enough evidence for me to take this any higher than this office."

"Father, I have seen the evidence myself and so have you. Even Father Chastain was there with you."

"I saw nothing. A young boy leaped from a balcony to his death. The last time I checked, that is suicide and frowned upon within the church. The boy was mentally unstable. Nothing more."

"But Father Dominic…"

"Enough! I will listen to no more of this nonsense."

Father Dickinson stood to leave when the phone rang. He walked to the door to exit the office and paused.

"Yes. I see. I will assign someone immediately, your Eminence." The Father hung up the phone. "Father Dickinson, your prayers have been answered. The church is taking up the case, and I have been told to cooperate. Do you have anyone in mind to help while the archdiocese chooses an appropriate priest to perform the exorcism?"

"Perhaps myself, as I am familiar with the family?" Dickinson answered, turning back to face his superior.

"The assistant for the exorcism will be for the exorcist to decide. For now, you will be the liaison for this. Behind the scenes, so to speak. I expect no problems and to have this issue resolved as soon as possible. Demons. Foolishness. You may leave. And Father?"

"Yes?"

"I'm not sure who you know, but I do not appreciate you going over my head on matters such as this."

"I assure you, Father Dominic, that I did not, nor would I ever attempt to do such things."

"Leave."

Father Dominic watched the young priest leave and close the door. The last thing the man wanted or needed was a possession within this diocese that became public knowledge. As far as the demon was concerned, Father Dominic had dealt with one of them in the past and knew the dangers involved. He had chosen not to indulge his young priest in these facts. It was not the time to do so.

CHAPTER 17
Silence from the Darkness

Rolland Brambilla cursed under his breath for the fifth time as the Portunus tried and failed again to grasp the maintenance handle of the U-116 forward hatch. The newly re-engineered arm installed by the MIT team was not living up to its hype. Shay Farley, the pilot of the robotic mini-sub, was equally frustrated as she tried to maneuver the Portunus in various positions to improve the angle on the target.

The new attachment was a claw not dissimilar to its predecessor, other than it being smaller, which in theory would enable it to reach into smaller spaces. The intended target was a handle partially obscured by the hatch it had been designed to assist in opening. A handle designed for a human hand, not a mechanical claw. "Damn engineers," Tarpon said, slapping his fist into the palm of his hand.

"The Germans did not want the possibility of the hatch snagging on anything unintentionally. It is quite well designed." Brambilla remarked.

"Well, we need another solution. Any ideas, Dr. Laurent?" Tarpon asked the MIT team leader.

"Let me take some time with my team to brainstorm. There has to be a solution to this."

"Time is one thing we are running short of, Doctor," Brambilla stated.

"Understood. Shay, let us get the Portunus up to the surface and get the team together. We have work to do."

"You got it, " the pilot replied and began preparing the robot for its return to the surface.

"In the meantime, Roli, you and I should resume our examination of the hull."

"I, for one, would also like to examine the pressure hull beneath the superstructure of the submarine. Perhaps we can if the hatches are open." Brambilla answered.

Five hours later the entire MIT Portunus team gathered in the conference room aboard the Scion of the Seas. Dr. Laurent was adamant that every team member be present, as she wanted all viable solutions, no matter how far-fetched they might be. Twenty people in all were comprised of deck volunteers, technicians and other highly skilled individuals that made the operation of the Portunus possible.

"This is the problem." Dr. Laurent began showing a video of the failure of the minisub's attempt to grab the handle of the hatch. "Our target is small and partially obstructed by the hatch itself. We need to produce a way to hook onto the hatch."

"Why?" One of the deckhands asked.

Laurent turned off the camera and leaned on the desk looking over her team. "To confirm a theory for this project and, most importantly, to prove that the Portunus is a viable tool in marine archeological research. What we have worked for is at stake, and we have to deliver. Failure is not an option. Otherwise, the future of the Portunus Project is at risk."

"What if we re-engineer the tool?" A young technician asked.

"Not enough time." The doctor rebuffed the student.

"Maybe a secondary tool the claw could use?" Another student asked. "You know, like something we might use for leverage?"

"Difficult. The claw is designed to do what it does, not to hold and utilize another tool." Clay Setzer said. Setzer was one of the lead designers of the Portunus and considered the minisub his brainchild. Dr. Laurent had leaned on the young man for his intelligence from the beginning of the project, which was to design the most sophisticated submersible robot ever built. The kid was a pure genius with robotics and had been since he was a child. Graduating high school three years early he was dubbed the prodigy of the new robotic age. Laurent had stumped tirelessly at MIT to get the kid on her team. She had finally resorted to using her own allotted scholarships and her influence to convince his parents that MIT was the right choice for the boy. The results were astounding throughout the four years of the project.

"I just don't see how we can do this without rebuilding the claw," Clay stated.

"Perhaps there is another way." Will Barnhart said. The Texan had joined the team as the chief mechanic for everything not associated with the actual robot. He was an expert on getting the machine in and out of the water and not having it destroyed. The forty-eight-year-old was an Army Corps of Engineers veteran both while in the military and once discharged into the civilian world. He knew his mechanical engineering inside and out. Levers and leverage were one of his specialties. "Perhaps a simple pry bar."

"What? C'mon Will. That is insane."

Dr. Laurent shushed Clay. "Go on, Will."

"I don't know robotics like the rest of y'all, but I do know something about mechanical devices. The Portunus is a robot and is made up of computer circuitry, cameras, and a lot of things that I know nothing about. But it does have mechanics, and that arm is a mechanical attachment. It has welds, nuts, bolts, and pins that hold it together. Driven by computer chips and advanced hydraulic systems that again, I know nothing about. The claw is quite simple. What if we augment it with a pry bar? Another piece of metal that it can hold and push into place. If successful, the leverage of the bar could be applied by the Portunus to manipulate the hatch. We are only trying to verify it is open and not sealed shut, right?"

"It's brilliant and simplistic." Another young researcher said. "Give the tool an additional tool. NASA has been doing it for years."

"I like it," Laurent said. "What about the tool?"

Will reached into his coveralls and tossed an open-ended wrench onto the table. Rounded on one end and the other bent at a fifteen-degree angle. I made this myself to work on the Portunus lockdown system on the deck. It seems that the engineers that designed the locking system did not consider how to properly access the securing system of the base." He said, smiling slyly at Clay.

Laurent ignored the comment. "How do we attach it?"

"We have a couple of options. The two I am considering take little time and could work. One is welding the pry bar onto the claw which I can do easily. The other is for the Portunus to carry it down to the bottom." Will explained.

"I am not a fan of the robot carrying it down. What if the pilot screws up and drops it?" Clay said, looking at Shay. "No offense."

"None taken, Clay. Jerk." Clay stuck his tongue out at his girlfriend.

"Stop it." We all have our jobs to do, so let's get to it." Dr. Laurent scolded. "Weld this thing on, and it had better stay, Will."

"My welds don't break."

"Fine, but I want a second prybar that the claw can grab just in case. Got me?"

"Yes, ma'am." The team said in unison.

"Good. Now everyone get to work."

Cathy was angry with her husband as she climbed into his pickup truck. The trip to the top of Mt. Washington had been spectacular but cold. The winter coats that Bill had brought for their getaway had worked perfectly and the views of the fall foliage had enlightened her heart. Then Bill told her about the true reason for the phone call from Clare. "I can't believe that you lied to me."

"Honey," Bill pleaded, "we were halfway up the mountain. What was I to do, tell you, and watch you jump from the train?"

"I could have handled it."

"Really, babe? OK, it's my fault. I should have spoken up, but I wanted us to have a few hours of happiness for ourselves. Besides, I was worrying enough for the both of us. I still am. I am really sorry."

"You are a complete jerk," Cathy said, punching her husband in the arm.

"That's me," Bill answered, starting the truck. "William Jerk Pender."

Cathy crossed her arms. "Let's go."

Gaea hung up her call with Lillian for the second time and was unhappy. She had trusted that the woman would keep her word and would not speak to her parents. In part, she did, yet she had called Clarissa, who in turn called her parents, who were now undoubtedly upset and angry. The girl understood why they would be with what was happening at the manor, yet she had really wanted a weekend of peace. It had ended in utter chaos for all parties. All except for her sister and brother. Even Bob Pepper had been involved in what was going on. She had been too young to realize that her 'adopted' grandpa had a hand in what had happened when Jack had died. After her impromptu meeting with him and listening in on his conversation, his involvement was apparent. Not knowing what to do, she went outside of the mansion and called her mother.

"Hello?" Cathy answered.

"Mom, I'm sorry."

"Sorry for what?" She said, trying to temper her voice.

"For ruining yours and Dad's weekend. It is just that I talked to Aerin."

Cathy could tell that Gaea was on the verge of tears as the girl's voice began to break up. She looked at the concern on Bill's face and shook her head and mouthed the word Gaea. He nodded. "You haven't ruined anything. Your father and I have had a wonderful time. It's not your fault what is happening at home."

"Me and Jack didn't get rid of it. What if it hurts someone else?" Gaea sobbed. "I can't do this alone, Mom."

"No one is asking you to honey. We are going to get some help." Cathy reassured her daughter.

Bill had pulled over to the side of the road and listened to one-half of the conversation. He was sure he could guess the other half. He took the phone from his wife's hands. "Baby, it's Dad."

"Daddy, I'm sorry."

"Don't be. There is no need. Look, Gaea, we are leaving the White Mountains now and are coming to Bar Harbor, so stay there, OK?" Cathy looked at her husband and smiled.

"Why come here?" Gaea asked.

"We will talk about all of this and figure it out. I think doing it at Bob's is better than at home."

"OK, Daddy. How long will it take for you to get here?"

Bill looked at the clock on the dashboard. It read 11:00 AM. "We should be there around dinner time. Five-ish or so."

"I'll let Vicky and Aerin know."

"And Gaea?"

"Yeah, Dad?"

"Ask the Peppers to plan on two more guests for a couple of days."

"OK. Miss you and love you." She said.

"We love you too," Bill replied and hung up.

"Thank you for that," Cathy said, leaning over and kissing him. "I was going to suggest that we go to Bar Harbor."

"I was figuring that you would want to go and be with the kids. A couple more days away as a family will do us all good."

"I think it will, too. we really do need to figure out what to do. In the meantime, can you call Mrs. Douglas and let her know we are extending our time away?" Bill said, pulling the truck back onto the road.

"Sure thing. I'll call Clare as well."

CHAPTER 18
Cracks Within Theories

Clarissa paced her home office trying to process what was happening over at Shaw Manor. She was no medium and had no special abilities herself, but she believed in them. She had seen the paranormal firsthand and witnessed what could happen when dealing with it. Thankfully, her husband Doug also not only believed in such phenomena but now had made it his career. The switch he had made by taking the position as Professor of Psychology and Parapsychology at the University of Southern Maine had been a shot in the arm for their marriage. The constant trips to New York were hell, and even with the birth of their son Logan, things had deteriorated between the couple as their careers were driving a wedge between them. Time away from one another and the stress of work was taking its toll on them. When Doug approached Clare with his plans of redefining his career after the incident with the Penders, she was all for it. The move up to Cape Neddick and his taking a new position had made her ecstatic. Everything had been going smoothly until the latest developments with her star writer and his family.

For reasons partially unknown to her, Clarissa felt somewhat responsible for the happenstances that were occurring around her. She knew this was not true. However, the feelings of unrest persisted. With Gaea growing into a young adult and with the birth of Aerin, along with the new occurrences at the manor, red flags had sprung up in Clare's mind. The more she talked to the children, the greater her concern became.

The phone call from Cathy had set her mind somewhat at ease. The only people at the manor were the housekeeping staff and the groundskeeping crew, who did not reside in the home. She had not, however, told Clare when the family might return. For now, they would all be up in Maine visiting the Peppers, and that was fine with her.

Clarissa simply could not comprehend why the demon that had caused the death of Jack Jefferson was still in the manor. For what reason? Did it want a family member? Aerin or Gaea, perhaps? The brother and sister did have abilities that might threaten the demon. Or did Belphegor simply want one or both for his own devious purpose? Clare simply couldn't comprehend the situation that she was once again part of. Grabbing her coat and keys, she headed out the door. Maybe Lillian had some answers.

It took Cathy and Bill nearly six hours to drive to Mt. Deseret Island and the Pepper Mansion. Traffic had been bad with the vast numbers of people going to and coming from viewing the fall foliage in the White Mountains of New Hampshire. Once back in Maine, the color explosion continued as they drove along the back roads of the western part of the state. Arriving on the island, Bar Harbor did not disappoint. It was equally as spectacular as where they had just visited. The difference was the addition of the Atlantic Ocean as a background to their perfect picture-postcard real-life painting.

"We should have just come here," Cathy said, taking in the view.

"Where else can you get mountains and the sea with a view like this?" Bill replied. "But we needed time just for us."

She rolled the window down, letting in a frigid blast of air. The salty scent hit her nostrils like the smell from an early morning bakery—irresistible and delicious. "Winter is on its way," she said.

"That it is," Bill replied, reaching over and turning on the truck's heater.

"What are you doing?"

"If you're going to freeze us out, I'm turning on some heat." He said, smiling.

"Fine," Cathy said, rolling up the window. "We're almost there anyway."

The couple were passing through downtown Bar Harbor. Most of the shops were closed, although a few were holding on past Columbus Day, which was the official end of the tourist season. "Hey, look!" Bill exclaimed. "The Floured Apron is still open. I could really go for a fresh blueberry pie."

"Vicky will be pissed," Cathy remarked. "Choosing another's pie over hers."

"C'mon, how angry can she get? It's only a pie."

The Portunus pilot had manipulated the mini-subs robotic arm perfectly, and the welded-on wrench slid into position on the handle of the U-116 forward escape hatch.

"It fits," Tarpon said, staring at a monitor on the bridge of the Scion of the Seas.

"Let's see if it holds," Brambilla added.

"We only have so much thrust, but it should be enough to confirm whether or not the hatch has been opened." Shay Farley informed them while manipulating the robot's remote controls.

She pushed a small lever on the control panel forward, activating the propellers of the Portunus. With her other hand, she used the leverage of the robotic arm to pull up on the hatch. It swung open. Cheers erupted on the bridge of the Scion of the Seas, which were immediately followed by silence. Everyone knew what may have just possibly been proven. The intentional sinking of a boat meant lives, and the fact struck home with the bridge crew.

The other two hatches had proven to be the same. All three hatches of the U-116 had been intentionally left open. The question now became, what happened to the boat's crew? Both Tarpon and Brambilla theorized that the crew had been evacuated and the officers had scuttled the submarine. Still, the scientists had questions that led to doubts.

"It's not conclusive, Jeffrey," Brambilla argued that evening. "We need to examine the pressure hull. Who is to say that the depth it sank to did not blow those hatches?"

Tarpon sighed and picked at his salad. "It is at crush depth, Roli. Not explosion depth."

"If it was sinking or going to sink, perhaps the crew tried to escape. If so, they would open the hatches and try to make it to the surface even if it caused the boat to flood."

"How do we prove it?"

"We cannot," Tarpon said. "I would not think the captain left any written logs behind, and even if he did, they have long been claimed by the ocean."

"We have come so far." Roland Brambilla said.

"We are out of time, Roli. But we have found the boat and have enough data to last the winter. We can come back in the spring."

"Why would we?"

"We have not examined the pressure hull. That might provide us some more answers." Tarpon received a text message and stood up to read it.

"What is that?" Brambilla asked.

"The museum in Bath is ready for us. They want to unveil the Shaw exhibit sooner than expected. Over a month early."

Brambilla rubbed his temples. "This is indeed early, Jeffrey. We will have to call Dr. Van Buren. She was a big part of Constance's discovery. No doubt she will want to be at this."

"No doubt," Tarpon answered. "And Bill Pender as well."

Vicky was livid. "What is that!? " She exclaimed, pointing at the box her father had set on the kitchen table.

"I told you," Cathy whispered to her husband.

The oven alarm sounded loudly, and Vicky turned it off. Reaching in, she pulled a fresh, hot blueberry pie from the oven and set it on the counter. "I made this for you, Daddy. You cheated on me."

Bill looked miserable as he took the purchased pie, walked over, and put it into the freezer. "I'm sorry, baby."

Bob Pepper stood at the kitchen's edge and laughed heartedly.

"What's so funny?" Vicky asked.

"I have never had the pleasure of having a child of mine yell at me. This is wonderful! Dottie does a grand job at it, but to have your child angry because you screwed up." He chuckled again.

"Grandpa," Vicky said, crossing her arms.

"Honey," Bob said, walking over and hugging her. "Trust me, we screw up, but our intentions are always good. Look how miserable he looks." Bob could barely control the tears from his laughter, and it caused Vicky to smile and then laugh.

"OK. But for now, I am the head chef around here, " she said, walking over to hug her dad. Bill rolled his eyes and looked at the ceiling as he hugged his adopted daughter.

"Bill, come up to my office." Pepper broke in. "We need to talk."

"Sure thing. Am I OK here now? I am not going to be forced to sleep out in my truck or something, am I?"

"Just go, jerk," Vicky said, returning to the oven.

"There is that word again," Bill said, following Bob. "What is she making anyway? It smells delicious."

"What is going on, Bob?" Bill asked, plopping down in the chair opposite his former boss.

"You have problems at home," Pepper said simply.

"It seems so, and they are not so simple."

"It's back, isn't it?"

"That would be an accurate assessment. I have a very gifted daughter and a son that apparently has a greater one."

"I'm not sure I would call it a gift, Bill. More like a damned curse if you ask me."

"Nothing I can do but try to help them deal with it," Bill said. "Anything to drink up here? I could go for a beer."

Bob pressed a button on a console that was built into his desk. "Yes, sir?" A voice came through a speaker.

"Henry, can you bring up a beer for Mr. Pender, please?"

"Right away." The man replied, and the com clicked off.

"I don't keep a wet bar in my office anymore. There's no need to, and if I want a soda or something, I get it myself. Exercise," Bob said, patting his stomach.

Bill nodded. "Don't I know it? My office is another story higher than yours." Henry came with the beer. Bill thanked the man and watched him leave. "Nice having a butler."

"He is a good man. He actually came with the place, as did most of the staff. We didn't know about it until after we bought the mansion. The former owner's husband died, and the wife moved to Florida to be with her sister. It left these folks in a bit of a bind. Nice bunch of people, and Dottie insisted on keeping them on."

Bill took a sip of beer and set the bottle down on a coaster on the desk. "So, why did you call me up here, Bob?"

"I've called in some help."

"Oh? What sort of help?"

"The sort of help that will kick that sonofabitch out of your house for good."

"I'm listening."

Bob stood up. "Come with me and bring your beer." Bill followed as Bob led him down to the first floor and into the east wing of the building. The mansion was huge, he thought, as after a lengthy walk, they stopped in front of a pair of closed doors. "This is my library," Bob said, opening the doors and motioning for him to enter.

The library was ten times the size of Bill's small tower in Cape Neddick, and the walls were lined with shelves, all of which were packed with books. On the far side of the room, a man stood before a window holding a book in his hands, which he closed when the two walked in. He was dressed in a black suit, and Bill had a tough time seeing him due to the dim lighting. When Bob turned up the lights, it became apparent that the man was a priest.

"Bill, may I introduce you to Father Sebastian Setzler, a priest of the Roman Catholic Archdioceses of Boston and an ordained exorcist."

CHAPTER 19
Plans & Prime Rib

Dr. Mary Van Buren had spent the last year and a half working in the Mediterranean Sea investigating a Greek merchant ship that had sunk during a storm over two thousand years ago. The Greek government had requested her assistance on the project through Dr. Roland Brambilla as he was unavailable due to his commitments in the North Atlantic with Dr. Jeffrey Tarpon. The choice had been a good one for the project and it had wrapped up nearly six months early. Van Buren still had to author papers and was considering drafting a book as well, so a year off to herself sounded quite nice. However, a winter in Canada did not. Perhaps a sabbatical in Hawaii would be appropriate. Then Dr. Tarpon called.

"Mary! Good to hear your voice. Can you come up to Maine? We would like you here for the ribbon cutting for the Constance exhibit." Tarpon spoke cheerfully in her ear.

"I would love to." She answered. "I was planning on heading over to the Hawaiian Islands for the winter to write my findings, but I guess it can wait. How is the weather in Maine?"

"Balmy for the fall." He lied.

"So, it's cold as a witch's tit on Halloween night." She said, chuckling.

"Well, yes. It is out here on the boats. We are wrapping up our project for now and heading for Bath and dry dock. At least the Archaean Horizon will be in for some work. We are not sure about the Scion of the Seas. We might have a short project in the Gulf of

Mexico to take a look at. It seems that another WWII U-boat has been discovered in relatively shallow water. Interested?"

"What is it with you and Roli and this new passion for warships?" She asked, taking a bite of pita bread. She had developed a taste for the native loaves of bread along with the Tzatziki sauce that the crewmen seemed to adore more than life. She had to admit that she did enjoy the light cucumber mixture. "And when are any of your projects short? But I might be interested after I finish these papers."

"A wreck is not always a simple one. Mary, you are always welcome on our team. Anyway, we are wanted at this ribbon cutting. Can you make it?"

"Who is paying?"

"I will, along with the museum. They really want you there for this." Tarpon pleaded. "As do I. We can stay on the Scion of the Seas. Wait until you see this boat. Top of the line, including the suites for the officers and researchers. And don't worry, no helicopter rides. She will be tied to the pier."

"In that case, of course, I will come for this. This project is wrapped up, so I'm taking some time off anyway. Have you talked to Bill Pender?"

"He is my next call after I get off the phone with you. I hope he will make the effort because without him the exhibit would not have been the success that it has become."

"True. He was incredibly generous with donating those captain's logs. They were invaluable to our research. Bill Pender not being there would be unfortunate, to say the least."

"When you are ready to travel, let me know, and I'll create the itinerary and send you the ticket."

"Sound's great, Jeff. I can't wait to see the two of you."

Tarpon hung up and smiled. He dialed Bill Pender and got his voicemail. "Dammit." He would try later.

"This is delicious." Father Setzler said, taking another bite of the prime rib that he had been served. "I don't think I have tasted better in my life."

"Thank you," Vicky said, standing near the door leading directly into the mansion's kitchen and wiping her hands with a towel.

"My daughter made all of this," Cathy said, smiling. "Her dream is to be a chef."

"She already is, without a doubt." The priest said, taking a drink of water. "You, my dear, are a rare find indeed. Perfect as this medium rare beef is."

"Wait until you try her dessert," Bill added taking a drink of his beer.

"Grandma Dottie helped me a lot," Vicky spoke up. "Without a proper sous-chef, it's hard to cook for a lot of people."

Dorothy Pepper smiled broadly and finished off her helping of sweet potato. "Really, this is all Vicky."

"Grandma, " the girl said, sitting down next to her sister. You are the best in the kitchen." This was one of the rare times that Vicky actually joined her guests at the dinner table. With the large staff the Pepper Mansion had, she was able to leave the serving of the food to them and enjoy the meal with her family.

"That's my sister." Gaea chimed in.

"Yeah!" Aerin said excitedly.

"Well, all I can ask is, where is dessert?" The priest said with a broad grin.

The dessert was as delicious as the main course. Vicky had baked four low-bush blueberry pies, and their sweetness exploded in the diners' mouths. The homemade whipped cream, along with the farm-fresh vanilla ice cream, only added to the experience. Aerin had made a minor complaint that it was not chocolate ice cream, but after a bite, he was all smiles.

"Remind me to give that pie I bought away," Bill said, rubbing his full stomach. "There is no way it will compare to this."

"Daddy," Vicky said, "they make great pies. I just wanted you to taste mine."

"And it is divine." Father Setzler spoke up. "None better in my life."

Vicky blushed and stood, picking up her plate. "Um, I best go to the kitchen. My mess, I will clean it up." Vicky stated firmly. She did, however, accept the offer of help by Aerin and Dottie. The wait staff of the mansion had been dismissed shortly after the prime rib had been served as per Vicky.

Mrs. Douglas was doing her daily walk-through of Shaw Manor with her two maids in tow. As it always went, after the daily cleaning was done, the head housekeeper inspected the work of her subordinates to make sure it was up to the standards that she and the Penders expected. With the family away, the cleaning had been rather easy. Taking care of the dog as well as the kitten had proven to be a minor inconvenience as the staff lived in the manor. As it turned out, Piddles had opted to sleep with Mrs. Douglas, and Licks chose to sleep with Piddles. The sleeping arrangement had been somewhat difficult for the older woman in the beginning, having only a full-sized bed, but she found she quite enjoyed the company of the animals. It had been years since she had owned her own cat, and she had never had a dog. Sleeping with both was quite delightful, although she would never admit to such a thing.

Karen and Chrystal had other thoughts but kept silent. The normally stern woman, who was their boss, was melting in front of their faces, and it was due to two cute pets that didn't know that the woman could turn into a marine drill sergeant at the drop of a hat. Still, the two girls couldn't deny the change in Mrs. Douglas's demeanor over the last few days. The new cordial attitude that the woman was showing to the two girls was welcome. The door that led up to the maid's quarters had been ordered to be left open and Mrs. Douglas herself had taken up the duty of feeding the animals and had taken charge of Piddles walks as well.

"The dog needs a firm hand and proper training." She had explained this to Karen and Chrystal. What the two suspected was that the daily walks from the manor down to the main road brought immense joy to the older woman.

The only thing that kept Shaw Manor from being a quiet lovely home was the knocking that came from the attic. It was not happening consistently, but when it did, it was loud and usually occurred at night. Since the maid's quarters were adjacent to the attic, having been built within the space, the only room that separated the women's bedrooms and the void was a shared bathroom. The few feet of space did not quiet the ruckus that came from the attic.

Mrs. Douglas claimed that the noise was from the pipes in the old house. The two girls did not buy the explanation and whispered their fears of a haunting among themselves. "Pipes, my ass." Karen had said to Chrystal one night as the two sat on Karen's bed. "Have you heard the voices?"

"Yes. It whispers and sounds like a girl. I think she is calling for help."

Cathy, Gaea, and the three men retreated to the library to discuss the problems facing the Penders and Shaw Manor. Gaea had been adamant about being included as she believed that she knew the most about what was happening in the manor.

"So, Gaea, I understand that you are a medium?" Father Setzler asked.

"Yes." She answered indifferently. "What does a priest know of it?"

The older man ran his hand through his gray hair and looked up, smiling. "I have the gift as well."

The girl looked at the priest in shock. "I thought that the church frowned on this like it was some sort of witchcraft or something."

Bill, Bob, and Cathy listened in with interest as Father Setzler continued. "On the contrary. Perhaps some members of the clergy do but there are some like me and Father Dominic that do not." The priest shifted in his chair. "I believe it a gift from God to help the deceased find their way to the gates of heaven. Some souls become confused, some become lost, and there are some that simply refuse to pass on. I believe I was given this gift to help these lost souls."

"And the possessed?" Bill asked, breaking in. "You are an exorcist."

"I am recognized as such by the church, and I am also a psychiatrist. I do believe in the clinically insane as well, and in cases such as those, exorcisms are rarely warranted, nor are they needed.

In this case, I see no one in need of a psychiatrist. At least not as of yet."

"Why is it only the Catholic Church that performs such rituals?" Bob asked.

The priest smiled. "Make no mistake, my brother. Faiths that believe in a higher power perform the ritual to banish evil as well, although by many different names. The devil does have many names throughout the faiths of the world and has many servants to help him spread his evil. In Christianity, we call him Satan, a fallen angel cast from heaven by God along with other angels. In Islam, its name is Iblis, and both represent evil and the eventual destruction of mankind."

"What about demons, Father?" Cathy asked.

"A demon is nothing more than a fallen angel who has been cast from the grace of God. It can be immensely powerful, however, and difficult to banish from the living."

"What if it takes over an inanimate object or a dead person?" Gaea proposed. "Is that possible?

"There are books on the subject, concerning demons possessing objects, in the archives of the Vatican. I have read these volumes. As far as possession of the dead, I can say that I believe that to be possible. I have a theory that if a demon desires to possess a person to claim their soul, and that individual dies with the demon possessing them, then the beast can retain possession of the soul and not allow its entry into the light. It has not been proven or accepted by the church, however."

"Jack," Gaea said softly.

"I have been told of the statue and the boy's sacrifice to destroy it." Father Setzler said, standing and walking to the window. "The story ends there. Are you telling me the demon was not banished?"

"No," Gaea said simply.

"By any chance, did you discover its name?" The priest asked, turning to face the girl.

"Belphegor." She said under her breath.

"What, my child? I did not hear that."

"Belphegor." She said loudly. Father Setzler stumbled back and slouched into his chair.

"You know of him, Father?" Bob asked, leaning forward.

"I do." The priest admitted. "The Defiler. It cannot be. The one known as Moab is one of the Princes of Hades. An enormously powerful demon."

"What do we do?" Bill asked.

The priest sighed and stood back up. "Is anyone at home now?"

"Just our servant staff. An older woman and two younger girls." Cathy answered.

"It won't touch them," Gaea added. "It prefers boys, but Vicky was involved."

"She is correct. Moab is a shapeshifter and prefers to take on the guise of a beautiful woman to deceive men. He also prefers to defile them, and the younger, the better. We need to get to your home and evaluate what is happening there. I have a feeling I will not like what I find. We should leave as soon as possible. In the meantime, I will speak to Father Dominic and attempt to get an assistant to help. It is very possible that Vicky will be needed as well."

"I can help," Gaea spoke up.

"And you shall in your own way when the time is right. For now, you need to protect your brother as I feel it is he that the demon wants."

"Over my dead corpse!" Bill exclaimed. "Aerin stays here, and that is final!"

Father Setzler walked to Bill and placed his hand on his shoulder. "There will never be peace until we banish the demon for the last time. It will hide. It will be deceitful. Only the presence of your son in the home will force it to show itself so that we can fight it and defeat it."

"How can we be sure that Aerin will be safe?" Cathy asked, concerned.

"We cannot." The priest admitted. "Only God can assure that."

CHAPTER 20
A Family Trip & A Toque

Dr. Tarpon finally got through to Bill Pender once the Archaean Horizon was in dry dock and the Scion of the Seas was safely tied up to Pier B in the harbor of Bath, Maine. The slow trip up the Kennebec River had proven to be non-eventful for the Scion. The harbor master had sent a pilot out to guide the Horizon into an awaiting drydock. They were fortunate to get time from Bath Ironworks as most were taken by the US Navy. Due to the need for only minor repairs and simple hull cleaning and paint, as well as his contributions to the US Navy's own research, he had been granted a few scant weeks for repairs to the aging ship.

"It would really be a special thing if you could at least make an appearance, even for a short time." Tarpon pleaded over the phone to Bill.

"I cannot promise anything, but I will see what I can do. I'm up in Bar Harbor with the family, but we are planning to head home soon, and Bath is on the way."

"OK. We hope to see you there."

Bill hung up and went to find his wife. The ribbon cutting was a month earlier than expected, and although manageable, it was a distraction from the problems facing him and his family. He thought for a moment and decided it might be another welcome one.

Cathy was in the kitchen with Vicky and Dottie, sipping on a cup of tea while watching them prepare a loaf of bread for the oven. A dozen fresh dinner rolls were already cooling on the counter, and the scent of them floated through the mansion. Her adopted daughter was becoming a master chef, and Cathy was not looking forward to the day when she left the family to head off to culinary school. A few years later, the girl would own her first restaurant, bakery, or whatever she wanted. She simply was hoping that whatever Vicky chose would be close to home. Top chefs were made in New York City, she had argued, but time would tell. As it stood, Vicky had her heart set on Ferrandi Culinary Institute located in Paris, France. Then, she would make her mark in the big city. It made Cathy's heart ache to think that Vicky would travel overseas to attend a school. Nothing but the best for her children, though. She had already decided what they wanted to do with their lives; they would have the opportunity to do.

"Something smells really good," Bill said, leaning against the wall.

"Thanks, Dad," Vicky said, opening the oven door. She slid the raw dough into it and closed the door.

"Cathy," Bill began, "I think we need to head home soon. Like tomorrow. We have to take care of this crap."

"That soon?"

"Well, I am needed at the Maine Maritime Museum for the unveiling of the Constance exhibit. I'm not really into doing it, but since we contributed significantly to the exhibit and are all a part of it, I think we should attend."

"I'm not opposed to doing that, Bill," Cathy answered, looking up at her husband. "I'm in no hurry to get back to the manor, although I know we need to. I am worried about the kids."

"Let's hope that Father Setzler can come through with help. I'm getting tired of dealing with all of this. I just want it to be over."

"We can defeat it, Dad," Gaea said, walking into the kitchen with Aerin tagging along at her side.

"It's afraid of me." The boy added. "Can I have a cookie? Vicky just made some, and I bet they are still warm."

"What do you mean it's afraid of you?" Cathy asked.

"It lies and pretends it wants me, but I think it wants someone else." Aerin said, pulling the glass of milk that Vicky had poured toward himself.

"Who?" Bill asked, walking over and sitting next to his son.

Aerin shrugged and took a bite of his warm, soft molasses cookie. "This is really good, sis."

"Who?" Bill repeated.

"I don't know."

Bill shook his head and stood up. "I hope that Father Setzler will have some answers for us."

"Me too," Cathy said.

Chrystal was not sleeping well. She had begun to have nightmares that woke her up in the middle of the night. The dreams seemed to have been similar over the last couple of days. Something or someone was taunting her from the attic. She would climb out of bed, walk down to the main hallway, and find the door to the attic open. She would then walk up the stairs until she found herself at the top, where she would try the light, but it would not work. The only illumination came from the dim moonlight that shone in from the windows. Otherwise, the space was dark. She could see crates that were open, as well as a mannequin standing close to the top of the stairs. More boxes were placed throughout the attic randomly. It was the voice that came from the middle of the room that caused her to wake up in a cold sweat. In a low, deep voice, it growled out two words that terrified her: "Secondhand soul."

The first time it happened, she had awakened and charged into Karen's room, waking her friend. Karen had tried to calm Chrystal, telling her it was only a bad dream, but even she wasn't convinced that it was only a nightmare. Simply comforting her friend did not seem enough. Karen believed that Shaw Manor was haunted. So far nothing had come of it but bumps in the night. These nightmares were a new development, and it did not sit well with her. Chrystal was not a person to become overly excited about things. Since the two had been working together, Karen had found her to be very levelheaded. A bit goofy at times, but when it came down to practicality, the girl seemed to make decisions with thought. It was a trait that she really liked and one that was not dissimilar to Mrs. Douglas, who was always stern but fair.

Running a house the size of Shaw Manor was not an easy task. Three women seemed barely adequate for the amount of work that they performed. Mrs. Douglas was a master at organization, and the two girls thrived on it. Both had spoken of one day being in hotel management, and opportunities to have the kind of on-the-job training that had been offered to them by the Penders were priceless. Learning how to manage and run such a house was difficult at best.

The monetary responsibilities were immense and the day-to-day planning for the home and adjusting to the family's needs, let alone pets, were challenging. Some duties became routine, others, however, not so much. Cleaning was a simple task. The Penders did not have many guests, and when they did, it was simple. Vicky had become the chef of the house, and Bill especially had taken it upon himself to make sure what was needed in the kitchen was there. If he did not, then his daughter did.

One of the issues was Aerin. The boy seemed to be constantly getting into trouble. Numerous times, Karen had saved him from near death, especially on the east side of the manor. Thankfully, Mr. Pender had installed the wrought iron fence on top of the wall preventing the kid from falling to his death. The incident with the bathroom access hatch had nearly brought Karen to the point of putting her foot down. Luckily, Mrs. Douglas had done that. Karen also hated the woods around the manor and refused to chase the boy into them. The rumors of the cemetery terrified the girl. Especially overhearing that a woman was wandering about the property that could be a spirit. Now with what was happening within the manor, all of the happenstances made her more afraid of the attic.

Karen held her friend and stroked her hair until she slipped into sleep. She hoped that the nightmares would not come to her own dreams.

The drive to the city of Bath, Maine, was simple and scenic as their destination was south on US RT 1, and with the season being over, traffic was light. The city was northeast of Portland; however, it was a vital port for the state, and the people of Bath had a symbiotic relationship with the Port of Portland. Bath Ironworks had been building ships for the United States Navy for years. It also did repairs for other mariners and companies, many of which had boats that were moored in Portland Harbor. Bath also had a quaint downtown tourist area as well as hotels, guest houses, shops, and restaurants.

The girls followed in Gaea's Jeep, Bill taking the lead in his pickup with Cathy and Aerin. The family stopped a few times to take in the scenery and once for a snack and gas. A frost had caused most of the multicolored leaves to fall, and many of the trees were nearly bare of foliage. Winter was quickly approaching, and it could be felt in the air. Bill had chosen a small place called The Chicken's Coop as their first stop. The temperature was a balmy thirty-three degrees, and he soon discovered that neither Gaea nor Vicky had come prepared.

"Why is it so cold?" Gaea asked, stepping out of her Jeep and rubbing her bare arms.

Vicky followed suit with her own complaints directing them at her sister. "It's your fault. I wanted to bring something warmer, and you said we wouldn't need it." Gaea stuck her tongue out.

"Girls, calm down." Bill reached into the back seat of the truck and pulled two garments from a box. "Who owns which one?" The girls rushed over and grabbed the winter coats hurrying to put them on.

"Thanks, Dad." Vicky said, pulling the hood over her ears. The wind blowing off from the Atlantic Ocean was not helping matters.

"Mom, my ears are cold," Aerin said, clinging to his mother.

"Let's all get inside and have some breakfast. And look, there is a sign that says gifts. Maybe they will have a hat or something. Let's see. OK?" Cathy asked lovingly.

An hour later they all left the restaurant with full tummies and Aerin sporting a new toque. The hat was white with red trim and a matching pompon. A cardboard brim had been sewn into the fabric giving it an old-fashioned look that Bill had found hilarious. He thought it made his son look similar to the old cartoon featuring Andy Capp. A red maple leaf with embroidery that read "Canada" stood out prominently on the front of it. The wool head cover was slightly large for Aerin, and he had to keep adjusting it as it kept slipping down and partially covering his eyes. His sisters found the look funny as well and teased him until they were all back in their respective vehicles.

"You all are mean," Aerin said, taking off his hat and throwing it onto the seat next to him.

"It's the only one that they had, honey." Cathy tried to explain, hiding her own giggling behind her hand. Looking back at her son, she lost it and fully broke out in laughter. Pulling off the toque had left his hair standing straight up. Bill glanced in the review mirror and broke out in laughter, too.

"What's so funny?" Aerin asked. "I took it off."

Cathy turned and leaned back. She licked her fingers, ran them through his hair, and smoothed it into something that resembled what it was supposed to look like. "There. You are all fixed now." Aerin's look at his mother conveyed that he was not amused. He then began to play his video game.

"We have to find a hotel," Bill said, changing the subject. "The ribbon cutting is not until later, and I don't want to drive home tonight."

"OK, I think that is a good idea. Hopefully, there is still something nice open this late in the year."

"Most of the big chains will be open." Bill replied. "But I would rather find a nice bed and breakfast; much cozier." Cathy smiled at her husband and reached over to hold his hand.

Dr. Tarpon was relieved that Bill Pender had chosen to attend the ribbon cutting for the Constance exhibit. Without the author's help none of this would be possible. He had recently found out that Bill had made a large donation to the museum. Without the gift, not only would this exhibit not have happened, but others would have failed as well. Tarpon knew all too well what private donations meant when it came to non-profit organizations not funded by the government. Museums were not much different than his own research. Luckily, uncovering the lost was more interesting to others than displaying what had been found. At least for a time. Newly uncovered archeological sites captured the public eye for far less time than their discoverers: the archeologists who sought them or the scholars who studied them. Perhaps, the scientist thought, Bill might have friends who were willing to contribute to science. It was something to bring up at the reception after the ceremony. In the meantime, he was happy to be putting on his tuxedo and being accompanied by Dr. Brambilla and Dr. Van Buren. A few of the original crew of the Archaean Horizon, who had been present upon the discovery, were still members of the team and were excited to attend as well. Tarpon had invited as many of the members of the expedition as he could, yet many of them were now on other projects throughout the world.

"I hear Pender is coming?" Brambilla inquired, walking up to Jeffrey. He reached over and adjusted his tie. "Mary is coming up shortly. How are you feeling?"

"Nervous," Tarpon said, leaning against the bulkhead of the Scion of the Seas. The wind had picked up, and standing on the deck of a ship with its port side exposed to the east was not the best place to be. From their vantage point they could see the Archean Horizon sitting in dry dock.

"She will be fine," Roli said, putting his arm around Jeffrey. "Lots of life left in that one."

"I know." He replied with a sigh. "I just don't like these fancy events."

"You know that we need them."

"Yes, but nevertheless, I don't have to enjoy going to them."

"And what are you two mumbling about?" Mary Van Buren asked, stepping out onto the deck.

"Nothing as usual. You look stunning in that green dress."

"This rag?" She spoke. "It's just something I threw on."

"My ass," Brambilla answered. "You look like you are ready for the Miss Italia Beauty Pageant in Milano."

"Stop it, Roli." She said, feigning a blush.

"Can we just stop the bull and go?" Tarpon broke in.

The trio walked down the gangplank towards a limousine that had pulled up to the dock. As they entered the car, Brambilla whispered into Mary's ear. "He's nervous."

CHAPTER 21
The Tired Toad & A Ribbon Cutting

The two-car convoy entered Bath before noon. Bill did his best as Cathy gave him directions to the bed and breakfast that had been booked by making a quick call to Bob Pepper. If anyone knew how to find an open hotel, he was the one. It took him all of an hour to find and book it for the Penders. "Make a left up here on Washington Street," Cathy instructed, reading a map. "Then we need to look for Union Street on the right."

"How far?" Bill asked.

"Let me see. According to the map, Union Street is not far once we make the turn. The bed and breakfast is at the end of the street."

"Can you tell how far the museum is from the hotel?"

"Not far. I'm guessing but ten, maybe fifteen minutes at the most."

"Good old Bob," Bill remarked and turned onto Washington Street.

Bath seemed like a typical large town that repeated itself throughout the State of Maine. To Bill, it did. The street was simple and lined with lovely old homes divided by quaint shops and an occasional strip mall. If he did not know any better, he would have thought he might be driving through Wells. The city of Bath was larger, however, and that was evident by some of the larger buildings. They were not structures used for textiles as one might find in a town like Sanford but were built to support the seafaring folk of the area, mainly ship repair and fishing. The tourist industry had helped the booming community and having the Brunswick Naval Air Station close by added to its booming economy.

"Cute, but I think I like where we live better," Cathy said, looking out the window.

"It's not Bar Harbor or Cape Neddick, is it?" Bill asked, turning onto Union Street. "But it is a city." He checked the rear-view mirror and saw Gaea's Jeep following behind. Aerin had slumped over and was sleeping soundly.

Cathy read off the address, and within a few minutes, they pulled up in front of a three-story Victorian-style house painted white with light cream trim. A wide set of steps led up to a large wrap-around front porch adorned with an ornate wooden railing. Next to the steps was a statue of a large toad sitting on a toadstool painted brightly in green, yellow, and blue. A sign swung from a white post that read "The Tired Toad." "This is it!" Cathy announced.

Bill pulled into an empty parking lot, followed by Gaea. "Season's over." He remarked. "This place was probably packed a couple of months ago."

"Aerin put on your hat and coat; we're here." His mother said nudging her son out of sleep. He yawned and looked around sleepily. The girls had already gotten out of the Jeep and were pulling their bags from the back of it. The wind was not as strong here because other homes and buildings blocked the gale. Still, it was cold, and the family quickly bundled up to make the short walk to the guesthouse.

Once inside, they found themselves in a large cozy room that had a lit fireplace on one side. A reception desk sat on the other side with a closed door behind it. Another flanked one side of a staircase. A hallway ran along the stairs. The room they stood in was tastefully decorated with wallpaper that rose from the white wainscoting, and potted plants were placed throughout the space. A seating area was in front of the fireplace that consisted of a Victoria-era sofa and two matching armchairs. A woman stood behind the reception desk and smiled broadly as Bill approached.

"You must be the Penders." She said, raking her long blond hair back with her fingers. "Here are your keys. Three rooms were all booked and paid for. I just need an ID for the files."

"Paid for?" Bill asked, pulling his wallet from his pants pocket. He handed the woman his driver's license.

"Yes, by Mr. Robert Pepper."

"Bob again," Bill said to his wife, who was leafing through one of the brochures displayed on the desk.

"All of those are closed except for a couple of them." The woman said to Cathy.

"We are here for an event at the museum. We are not tourists. In fact, we live in Cape Neddick." Bill answered.

"Oh, I love it down south!" She said, handing Bill's license back to him. "My name is Trisha. I own this place along with my husband. Your rooms are down here on the first floor as we have closed the upstairs. We shut down after the season is over."

"I've lived near the coast all of my life," Cathy said, placing the brochure back in its holder. "Most of Maine shuts down in the winter. I am Cathy, and he is Bill. The kids are Gaea, Vicky, and Aerin."

"We live here in the house, and our bedroom is behind me," Trisha said. "If you need anything, just knock. Normally, I wouldn't tell my guests that, but since you are the only people here, I see no harm in it. We like to run a cozy guesthouse. By the way, I will be serving coffee, orange juice, and a continental breakfast in the dining room in the morning. That is the door on the other side of the stairs."

"Delightful," Bill said, turning to look for his children.

Gaea and Vicky were warming up next to the fireplace, and Aerin had made his way up the stairs to explore. An older man was carrying him back down, gently scolding him. "Upstairs is off limits, young man, " he said, setting the boy down at the base of the stairs.

"I'm sorry about that," Cathy said and went to her son. "Girls, why are you not watching him? You know how he likes to wander off."

"But Mom, there is a ghost upstairs that wants to talk to me," Aerin replied. "She said her name is Dorothy."

Trisha dropped the pen she was holding and came out from behind the desk. She went to Aerin and knelt. "Dorothy? Are you sure?"

"That is what she said."

"Did she look like that woman?" Trisha asked, pointing to a painting of a woman on the wall.

"Yeah, that's her."

Trisha stood up and walked over to a chair and sat down. "That is my mother. She died two years ago."

Clare was beside herself with concern about what might be happening at Shaw Manor, and her husband was helping to calm her nerves. Both had seen that which was capable of happening at the old home and she was terrified. Bill had mostly vanished on a vacation with his family, and she had been unable to reach Lillian. Doug had been brushing off the situation, yet she didn't believe he was completely telling her the truth. The man was supposed to be an expert in the paranormal, yet he kept telling her the same explanation. Pipes and bumps in the night and peaceful spirits.

Doug did indeed feel differently about the ongoing happenstances that were occurring at Shaw Manor. His protective instincts kicked in, and he kept silent and he feigned to be obtuse to the situation. He knew there was a serious situation at the manor, and he was determined to find the underlying cause of it. He had his own theories that mixed with the facts that had been presented by the people involved. The ones who knew what might be happening. The bottom line was that it was the paranormal, and nothing could be claimed as fact and left to speculation until proven. The scientific side of his brain was in constant battle with the skeptical fictional side.

"Try to call Bill again," Doug said to his wife.

"I have dozens of times. He never erases his voicemail, and most times, Bill does not even charge his phone. Not to mention he's an idiot at using that new iPhone he bought. He will not ask for help, either. Stubborn ass." She answered, slumping on the sofa and crossing her arms.

"Honey, let me try."

Bill drove Gaea's Jeep, and Cathy was visibly excited. Every museum excited his wife, and this one was no exception, especially since it involved her own home, Captain Shaw, and Constance. Having spent much of her life running a museum and then her own shops that dealt in antiquities, anything that was remotely related to something old drew her like a moth to a flame.

"This is going to be such a drag, Dad. Who cares about dead sailors and sunken boats?" Vicky asked.

"Your mother and me," Bill replied. "If it were not for Wilbur Shaw, we would not have the manor. And you yourself want to go to the Idaho Potato Museum."

Gaea rolled her eyes. "I'm out on that trip. Who wants to go halfway across the country to the middle of nowhere to look at potatoes? You are such a geek, Vicky."

"What about you wanting to go to that creepy paranormal museum in Louisiana?"

"Because that is cool." Her sister replied. "A baked potato is not."

"Okay, you two. Everyone has their own interests." Cathy said, turning and looking at her daughters. Aerin sat between them, engrossed in his video game.

"They didn't even take us with them to Story Land," Gaea said, glaring back at her mother.

"What!?" Vicky exclaimed. "I have wanted to go there all of my life and they left us out?" She crossed her arms and slouched, pouting.

"You? I have been promised Disney World since I was a kid and nothing, so who are the kids in this family?" Gaea said, reaching over and lightly slapping her father on the back of his head.

"Stop it!" He said. "We really need a Limo so we can shut those two in the back and not have to hear the bitching." Bill said, turning into the museum's parking lot.

"For sure," Cathy answered. "And maybe plan a family trip to Orlando, Florida."

"I just don't understand why Bill or Cathy won't answer their phones," Clare said to Doug. "There is a very serious situation over at Shaw Manor, and they are not addressing it."

Lillian had driven over and joined the Drakes to discuss the problem, and she was at a loss as well. The three sat in the living room when there was a knock at the door. Upon opening it, two priests greeted Doug, one older than the other. "Greetings. My name is Father Dominic, and this is Father Setzler. It seems that we have an issue to resolve."

The museum was everything and more for a wide-eyed Cathy. Vicky was also impressed by the displays. However, keeping Aerin in check proved to be an issue, as the boy wanted to run everywhere and touch everything in sight. A rope meant to separate a display from the public meant nothing to him as he barged through to look and feel. It finally took Gaea's scolding to make him calm down.

Vicky had found the exhibit area that portrayed the galleys of fishing vessels and had become enthralled with how the use of small spaces could be so functional. Gaea was completely bored but was trying to amuse herself at an exhibit depicting an old lobster boat that had been put on display after being salvaged. Cathy was running about, trying to take everything that the museum had to offer. Bill had found Dr. Tarpon and was being briefed on the ceremony that was to happen. He had been given a brief tour of what was to be displayed, and he had to admit that he was impressed. The exhibit was not large; however, it was presented beautifully, and the information was beyond expectations. Photographs of Captain Shaw and Lily were displayed over what appeared to be a replica of the Constance that someone had constructed as a model. Pictures of the wreck site adorned a section of the exhibit with interactive videos of the Archaean Horizon's expedition. Bill was most impressed by the deck log section. Every one of them was on display with a computer interaction that let the visitor browse through the pages electronically and be viewed on numerous monitors.

"Impressive," Bill said, looking over the artifacts that were displayed behind a glass panel. Above them on the wall was a painting of the Constance at sea, her sails unfurled.

"I think so as well," Tarpon said, pointing to the painting. "That is not actually the Captain's boat, but a rendition based upon what it could have looked like at the time. A few of that style were built but we have no way of knowing."

"A puzzle with too many missing pieces."

"Good analogy, Bill. But that is archeology in a nutshell, is it not?"

"You can speak to my wife about that."

"Speaking of her perhaps this might be the proper time to bring up something I have been contemplating for quite some time."

"Oh?"

Tarpon put his hands behind his back and looked at the author. "Whether to tell Cathy that she is my relative. A cousin, in fact. She and I used to play together when we were young, although I doubt she would remember." Bill stood stunned in front of the archeologist as Tarpon continued. "I grew up in Montreal, Canada, and during the summers, we would vacation in southern Maine, and once, we stayed with my mother's sister's husband. I remember that we went to this whimsical theme park called Story Land. The place scared me to death. Creepy."

"We went there just recently," Bill said. "I wonder if it brought back some memories."

"Memories of what?" Cathy asked, walking up and overhearing the men's conversation.

"Maybe I should let Dr. Tarpon explain," Bill said. Cathy looked at Tarpon curiously.

CHAPTER 22
The Withering Dawn

The morning at Shaw Manor broke with freezing rain coating the trees throughout the estate grounds. A brisk wind had made short work of the remaining leaves on the maple trees, and they now stood bare, awaiting the onslaught of winter and the snow. Mrs. Douglas sat with the two housemaids, having a breakfast of eggs, sausage patties, and mini blueberry pancakes topped with fresh butter and Vermont maple syrup.

"There is something up there," Chrystal said, taking a sip of orange juice.

"I keep telling you Shaw Manor is an old house, and the pipes creak." Mrs. Douglas answered.

"But pipes don't whisper and talk," Karen added. "I agree with Chrystal, and something is not right."

Mrs. Douglas stood up and took her plate to the sink, then turned to face the two. "The Penders are on their way home and will be here soon. I want clean sheets on the beds and a house that is neat and clean when they arrive. We will let them deal with these so-called spooks in the attic. Non-sense. All of it." She collected the girls' plates and placed them into the sink, watching them head off in separate directions to perform their assigned chores. She began to hand wash the few dishes. Looking out the window at the Atlantic, she sighed. She had heard the voices as well.

"Finally," Clarissa exclaimed. "Bill, I have been trying to call you for hours. Check that. Days. Where the hell are you?"

"Just leaving Bath. We had a ribbon cutting for the Constance exhibit at the museum up here."

"You know there are issues at the manor?"

"Yes. We have already spoken to the priest up at Bob's. He called them in to help."

"Well, they are here at my house along with Lillian. I suggest that you let us know when you are close to getting home."

Bill sighed and handed the phone to his wife. "I'm driving can you handle this?"

Cathy hung up after a few moments. "They wanted us to go to Clare's house and talk about how to handle this problem, but I wanted to get back to the manor. We will call them once we are back, and they will come to see us over there."

"This could get ugly, babe," Bill said, putting his phone back into his pocket.

"That is what I am dreading. I don't know if I can handle something like what we went through the last time. And I am terrified for our children."

"I told you, Mom. It doesn't want me. It wants someone else." Aerin called from the back seat.

"But who then?" Cathy whispered in frustration.

"I told you I don't know." He answered.

The two vehicles pulled into the manor driveway just before eleven in the morning. The freezing rain had changed to snow, and it was sticking as it hit the frozen ground. The estate was beginning to look like a winter wonderland. Bill pulled up near the front of the manor and stopped. Gaea did the same. "Let's unload, then we can call the cavalry," Bill said smiling.

"Not funny," Cathy replied, looking apprehensively at her own home through the falling snow.

Gaea and Vicky had already grabbed their bags and were at the front door being met by Mrs. Douglas. "Get in here where it's dry, and take your bags up to your room. Heavens, the weather has turned nasty."

"Nice to see you too," Vicky said, heading for the grand staircase. Gaea followed her sister. Aerin charged into the foyer next, followed by his parents, blew past Mrs. Douglas, and charged up the stairs.

"Everything okay?" Bill asked his head housekeeper.

She looked at the worry in Cathy's face and lied. "Nothing new. The house is still standing." She said, smiling. "I think you will find everything in order."

"We are expecting guests later. I don't know if it will be overnight. Do we have rooms ready?" Bill asked.

"Yes, Mr. Pender. All rooms are made up clean and ready, " the woman said, " as they always are."

"I'm sorry, Mrs. Douglas. You and the staff do a fantastic job. I don't know why I bother asking."

"You have the right as you are the master of the manor."

Cathy rolled her eyes and scurried by her husband. "I'm going to go change." She stopped short of the grand staircase and turned. "What are we doing for supper? I do not really want a big dinner deal for this tonight."

"I'm good with pizza," Bill said, shouldering his backpack. "I'm not sure Vicky will be, though. Let me check with her."

Father Setzler took another sip of his tea. "Earl Grey. Delicious. A splendid choice."

Father Dominic did not feel so calm and collected. "You take this situation far too calmly, Father."

"On the contrary, I do not. Dealing with a powerful demon is no trivial matter. But the slow and methodical approach is the best way to defeat this monster. I have done this more than once."

"That you have, Father Setzler. That you have my friend."

"I just wish the Penders would call," Clare said, walking to the window and looking out at the falling snow. The sun was setting, and a streetlight had come on, illuminating the snowflakes in amber light. "It gets dark too early in Maine this time of year."

"But it is a lovely time. Don't you like the snow?" Lillian asked.

"About as much as a toothache," Clare answered. "Except maybe for Christmas."

"Mom, I'm hungry," Logan said walking into the room holding his GI Joe doll. Doug came out of his office and picked his son up as Clare's phone rang.

"Thank goodness." She said before speaking into it. "Of course, Bill. We can all be there in a few minutes. We are all on edge here."

Clare said, eyeing the priests. "That would be perfect. OK. See you in a few."

Doug looked at his wife questionably and said, "I guess we are off to see the Penders."

"I am afraid I will be back later tonight. I must return home and tend to some other matters. I will meet you all there at the manor." Lillian said, standing up.

"I hope it's nothing pressing," Doug said.

"Nothing serious."

Clare nodded, looked at her son, and smiled. "Looks like pizza for supper."

"Yay!"

Vicky called in the pizza order to Luigi's and went to pick them up. She had been a little miffed that she was not being allowed to cook them herself. However, lack of time, as well as limited ingredients, made that effort an impossibility. Instead, she made it her responsibility that the quality of the order was up to her standards. One of the pies was slightly overcooked, to Vicky's dislike, but she let it slide. The snow fall was continuing, and it was getting late. Next time she would make the meal. Placing the five large pizzas on the back seat of her Jeep, she started the engine. Turning a knob to place the SUV into a four-wheel drive, she headed for home.

She brought the boxes into the kitchen and asked the family and guests, as well as the staff, to gather in the dining room. Paper plates and plastic cutlery had already been laid out on the table by Karen and Chrystal, but Vicky would not serve food in cardboard boxes. She placed each pie on a serving platter along with two triangular serving spatulas and brought them to the table with Karen's help. It was also decided that the staff would join the pizza party at the table at the behest of Father Setzler. This gathering would not only be a meal but also an information-sharing session.

Chrystal brought in bottles of soda as well as three bottles of red wine, which she opened to allow it to breathe, which was technically not necessary, Vicky noted as she watched. The practice of letting wine aerate had long been dismissed by sommeliers and wine stewards of the world. Simply swirling the wine in the glass gently would suffice to bring the full flavor to the taster. She let the culinary slip slide and took her seat next to Gaea. Chrystal began to act as a server before being told to sit down by Gaea. "You are not working this evening. Neither of you two are either." She said to Karen and Mrs. Douglas. "It is very important you are here with us."

"Well said." Father Setzler said, pouring a small amount of wine into his glass.

"Before we begin," Father Dominic said, standing up, "I believe we should give thanks for this meal we are about to sup."

"I'm not sure that is such a good idea," Gaea said.

"Nonsense." He responded and said a simple grace. A loud crashing sound came from above as he finished the simple prayer.

"You woke it up," Aerin said, taking a slice of pepperoni.

"It's pissed off," Lillian added.

Father Setzler looked up at Dominic. "Perhaps you should let me oversee this."

"Perhaps." He said, sitting back down.

"As we eat you will all speak your minds and tell me about your experiences with this demon. That includes the children. I need to know everything you have heard, seen, or experienced." Setzler explained, cutting a piece off his slice of Hawaiian pizza with a knife and fork.

"It was years ago when this all started." Cathy began, then continued to explain what had happened with the death of Tracy, the happenings at the manor, and bringing it all to an end, they had thought, by finding peace for Captain Shaw. Bill continued the conversation of bringing a possessed statue of Anubis into the house, which led to the death of Jack by his trying to defeat the demon that possessed it.

"What happened to Jeremy?" Father Setzler asked placing his napkin onto his plate. One slice of the pizza had been enough for the older man.

"He is living in New York City and wants nothing to do with this problem," Clare said, taking a sip of wine. "I called him."

"Fair enough." The priest replied. "He is not needed here and would only be in the way and possibly in danger."

"Father, the children," Lillian spoke up.

"It cannot be helped. They are part of this as well. I understand there are gifted people at this table. Please speak up if you feel you possess the gift." The priest demanded softly.

"I have the gift." Cathy offered. "But not so strong. The dead do not talk to me."

"A sensitive. Yes. Who else?"

"I am a medium," Lillian answered. "I have been one since I was a child."

"Who else?"

"Me," Gaea said. "I was the one that helped Jack to defeat Belphegor the first time."

"Do not say the fallen one's name here, my child. It is not the time. But yes, I can feel you are a strong medium but there is another at this table that is stronger than either you or me. Isn't that right, Aerin?"

The boy picked at his pizza and shrugged. "It's afraid of me."

Setzler stood up, walked around the table, and knelt next to the boy. "You are much more than a medium, aren't you, my child?"

Aerin looked at the priest, and his eyes changed from brown to blue and then back to brown. "It wants someone else." He turned back to eating his pizza. Logan saw his friend's eyes, stood up, and ran off screaming.

"The pizza party is over, and it is time to enter the lair of the beast." Father Setzler said, standing up. "Clarissa, perhaps finding your son is in order."

CHAPTER 23
Secondhand Souls

"I want Gaea and Lillian to go up with me for the first look." Father Setzler said, donning his purple vestment and kissing his blessed crucifix. He placed a vial of holy water in the pocket of his robe and picked up his well-used tattered Bible.

"Father Setzler, what about me?" Father Dominic asked.

"Yes, you also, but you must remain in the background until the actual exorcism begins. Then your presence will be much needed."

The father nodded and stepped back. "I am not an exorcist; nor do I wish to be one."

"The rest of you stay down here." The priest added. "Except for William and Douglas. You both will remain at the bottom of the stairs."

"Why can't Bill at least call me and let me know how it is going down in Cape Neddick?" Robert Pepper said aloud as he stormed around his office. He had nearly broken down and opened the bottle of scotch that sat on his desk, the seal still neatly attached to its neck. He had reached for his phone countless times, then fell back into his chair, thinking better of the idea. The situation was well in hand as he knew Father Dominic and Father Setzler were well capable of the task. Still being an ex-publishing mogul, he was used to being kept informed of all situations.

He stood and walked over opening the sliding glass doors and stepping out onto the balcony. The icy wind hit him in the face, but he ignored it and stepped further out into the cold. Snow was falling heavily, covering the tiled surface of the veranda. Bob let the cold sink into his body for a moment, then walked back inside. Maine was colder than his native New York, but he had an affection for Vacationland and was determined to spend the rest of his life in the most northeastern state. He picked up his phone and muttering, 'screw it,' he called Clarissa. A couple of rings later, she answered. "Hi Bob, what's up?"

"What's up?" He partially shouted into the phone. "Everyone I care about is down at the haunted manor and no one bothers to keep me up to date with progress?"

"I'm sorry, but we just had a dinner meeting, and they are getting ready to go upstairs, " she answered quietly.

"Who are 'they'?"

"Well, to start with, it is going to be Father Setzler, Lillian, a medium who you have not yet met, along with Gaea and Father Dominic. Our exorcist made the choices." She explained.

"OK, Setzler is a good man of the cloth, and I trust him. But Clare, can you keep me in the loop? This is killing me. I'm too old for this shit. And if anything happens to that girl, there will be the…, well let's just say I will not be happy." He finished, cutting off his words.

"Bob, I promise I will call you with every development from now on."

"OK. I'm just, well, concerned. Genuinely concerned."

"We all are Bob, we all are."

Bill unlocked the attic door and pulled it open. Reaching in, he flipped the switch on the wall, and the yellowish light bulb came to life at the top of the stairs, illuminating the small portion of the space that could be seen.

"Let me go first," Gaea said, stepping onto the first step.

"Me next," Lillian added.

"This is wise, " the exorcist commented. The demon will react when it sees us, perhaps most unfavorably," Setzler said to Father Dominic quietly.

"Perhaps, but God will defeat it."

"We are only men, but we live in the grace of God."

"Amen, Father."

The two women walked slowly up the stairs, followed by the two priests. Bill and Doug stood nervously at the bottom of the stairs and watched. As they reached the top, the light bulb shattered, and a low laugh came from the darkness.

Downstairs, Aerin looked up from the video game he was playing with Logan. "It's awake, and it knows that they are coming."

Cathy went over and sat by her son. "How do you know?"

He shrugged. "I can hear its thoughts. It's not happy."

Cathy looked at Clare, and her face was one of fear. "I don't want to do this again," Cathy said, walking to the kitchen and pouring herself a glass of wine.

Vicky stood nearby with a look of concern on her face as well. "Mom, she is my sister, and I feel helpless also. OK, so she is not my blood sister, but still."

"I know, honey. You are a part of this family and always will be."

Clare followed and hugged her. "I don't want to do this either. Can I have a glass?" Cathy smiled weakly and Vicky poured her a glass.

"I just wish I were more able. My own son is psychically stronger than I am, and he is a kid. And look at Gaea. If she hadn't helped Jack…and it was all my fault." Cathy broke down sobbing. "If I hadn't brought that statue into this house, none of this would be happening."

"You had no idea, Cathy. It was just a piece of art to you and nothing more." Clare consoled her friend by stroking her hair.

"They are in the attic," Aerin said, simply looking up before returning to his game.

Cathy and Clare looked at one another.

"You are not welcome here. Why do you come?" A voice croaked from the darkness of the attic.

"Why are you here?" Gaea asked searching the darkness with her eyes for the origin of the voice.

"That is of no consequence. I choose, so I am here."

"You are not welcome here," Lillian spoke.

"Again, of no consequence. I choose, so I am." It repeated in a low gritty voice.

Father Setzler joined them, illuminated a small flashlight, and began to scan the attic with it.

"I thought I smelled the stench of a priest." It spoke.

The priest cast the light toward the voice, and it lit up a chair twenty feet away. Gaea gasped. "That's Jack."

"No, it is not. The demon lies and takes the form of your dead friend."

The depiction of Jack, the demon he had become, was terrifying to Gaea. He appeared as some sort of perverted clown with black eyes, although a resemblance to the man who once lived was apparent. The fiery red hair was caked in blood that had turned a shade of brown, and a portion of its skull was caved in.

"Belphegor, show yourself." The priest commanded.

"I choose not to, and you have no power over me."

"I do not, but the Lord does, " he said, raising his crucifix toward the demon.

It feigned a lunge at Father Setzler, then fell back into the chair laughing. "It will take more than you, priest."

"I am here, Belphegor." Father Dominic said, moving to stand next to Setzler. "You cannot deny God, and you will release the souls that you have imprisoned in this house."

"The three are nothing more than secondhand souls and belong to me. They chose to take their own lives, and that so-called *sin* damned them. Thus, I claim their souls. They are mine, and I use them as I wish."

"Christ is the redeemer demon, and by his grace, we will save them," Setzler said.

"Give me the boy, and I will leave." It demanded.

"You can't have Aerin!" Gaea said angrily.

"Shut the whore up." It barked back. "It is not this man that I want. Give me the child called Logan."

"You will have no one and return what is rightfully God's property. You have no claim to them, for they have committed no crime."

"They took their own lives." It growled.

"That is a lie," Gaea said. "Tracy fell to her death by accident, startled by Rebecca. Rebecca died by disease, and Jack died trying to rid you of our home. Father Setzler is right. You have no claim to them. You stole them."

"Prove it." The demon laughed.

"There is no need, Belphegor. You will be cast out. Come, let us prepare."

It jumped from the chair and charged the group. Setzler, however, was prepared with an open vial of holy water and splashed it toward the demon. The demon screamed and vanished.

"Is it gone?" Gaea asked.

"No. it is simply hiding." The exorcist answered.

"The bastard wants my son?" Clare asked, horrified.

"He is the weakest among us who is male. Belphegor is a coward and uses shapeshifting to entice the living." Father Dominic said.

"He takes great delight in corrupting powerful men and lusts after children."

"Well, he is not getting Logan! Doug, take him home now." Clare demanded.

"Please, you cannot take him away. If you do, this all will continue as the demon will simply sit and hide until another opportunity arises. It will continue to reside in this house." Father Setzler added, walking to Logan and touching him lightly on his head. The boy glanced up for a moment and went back to playing the video game. "Time means nothing to the beast."

Doug came forward. "Wait, so you want to use him as bait?"

"No. That is not correct. I would say an enticement." Setzler began. "He will not be going anywhere near where the demon resides. That is for me and Father Dominic to do. Gaea, Lillian, and Aerin will also be needed for their unique abilities, but I suspect that they will be in no danger."

Vicky had heard enough and charged out of the kitchen. "What the hell does suspect mean?" She demanded. "You are talking about my brother and sister here, and quite frankly, this all sucks."

Cathy stroked Vicky's hair and kissed her. "I think I know what he is saying. But what is a secondhand soul? It does not sound pleasant."

"It is a term seldom used in the church, but I have come across it in literature." Doug offered. "The theory is that when a person dies, they have a choice to pass on, or they may choose to remain behind because of unfinished business in their lives or several other reasons. It is the time when the soul is most vulnerable to being usurped by a demon such as Belphegor. Once taken by the demon, the soul becomes trapped until it is released or it is rescued. Thus, it becomes a secondhand soul, or one being used."

"A pertinent description," Setzler commented. "And as far as I know, extremely accurate." Father Dominic nodded.

"I don't know much about this crap," Bill said, walking to the bar and pouring a shot of scotch, "but the title Father. Isn't that a high-up position in the church? Can't you just go up there and tell the thing to go back to Hell?"

"It's not that easy, Mr. Pender. Father Setzler, perhaps you can explain." He replied.

"Yes. You see, not even the Pope himself could do such a thing. We are all quite simple men and women in the service of the Church and God. We evoke the power of the Father, Son, and the Holy Ghost to do God's will. We all have specific chores that we do, but the hierarchy is for structure. Father Dominic has no training in the rights of exorcisms as his tasks are different than mine. He is my senior, and I must go to him for guidance, but without this structure, there would be chaos within the church. So, you see, if he were to attempt to try what you suggest, the demon would defeat him easily. I have spent most of my life training and performing the rights of exorcism to keep demons at bay. I cannot destroy a demon. Just banish it temporarily. Eventually, it will return to try to corrupt mankind again. There is only one that can destroy a fallen angel and that is God himself."

"So, this is an eviction?" Vicky asked, still not convinced. "What if it comes back?"

Father Setzler smiled as best as he could under the circumstances. "I have banished many demons, my child. In every case, none have returned to the location of the original possession. I believe that it chooses to go to another place where it is not known to do its evil deeds in secrecy. Once it is discovered, the cycle begins again. For this house, the demon was never banished, and it simply hid until an opportunity arose that let it start once again.

"The birth of Aerin," Cathy said softly.

"Perhaps." The priest said. "There is no way to tell."

"Can the demon take the souls with him?" Doug asked, pouring himself a glass of whiskey. "I mean, the three that are here in the manor?"

"I do not think so. I believe that at death, they are bound to the place where they passed. In this case, all three of the spirits died here at Shaw Manor."

"So, if we banish this piece of dung, the three souls will be released," Bill said, refilling his glass.

"They will be able to make the choice to pass on or to remain, however, they will not be bound any longer by the demon. Their free will can be restored, and their souls left intact."

"How powerful is Belphegor?" Clare asked.

Father Setzler sighed. "He is one of the princes of Hell. Once a powerful angel, he was cast out with Satan and the rest that opposed God's will. This demon is not to be taken lightly, and he has the ability to not only corrupt but to destroy a person to the point of death. He is deceitful and a pathological liar, so don't believe anything that is spoken from his vile mouth. Belphegor is also a shapeshifter, which is what was done this evening in the attic. He can take the guise of anything or anyone, although he prefers attractive, voluptuous women to seduce the men and boys he desires. In this case, he chose your deceased friend, Jack. Make no mistake, we could be in for a long and difficult battle to banish the demon."

"When do we begin?" Gaea asked.

"Tomorrow. It is late, and my strength is waning. Perhaps we can stay?" Setzler asked.

"We have rooms. Are you sure it's safe?"

"Oh, yes. The demon is not possessing a living human and has gone into hiding. Take Logan home and come back tomorrow. Everyone will be safe."

The house staff shuffled nervously near the kitchen, and Bill noticed. "You all can leave if you want."

"Not in your life." Mrs. Douglas said. "I am a part of this family, and I am staying where I am needed." Karen and Crystal nodded in agreement.

"I'm going to get busy cooking. If this is going to take a lot of time, there will be hungry mouths to feed." Vicky said, donning her apron and tying it.

"I'll help." Karen offered.

CHAPTER 24
Preparations

Bob had had enough and sat on his private jet as it prepared to land at the Sanford Municipal Airport. He had sent his limo the day before to meet him upon arrival. He just could not stand to be left in the dark when there was trouble brewing within his family and he considered the Penders his close family. Dottie had put up a fuss, but he had won out, and she agreed to stay at the mansion to take care of things.

"We are about to arrive." The flight attendant said. "Please fasten your seat belt."

"I don't need to be reminded." He told the young man and clipped the buckle together. Josh smiled and went to sit in his own seat. Bob sighed and looked out the window at the clouds below. A winter storm was building, and he could see sparse patches of land below; all of which were white. The jet slowed on its approach, and he could see snow blowing by the windows. "Perfect," Pepper mumbled. It touched down without issue and taxied to a stop near the limo on the tarmac.

"One moment, sir," Josh said, smiling.

Pepper rolled his eyes and stood up, grabbing his overnight bag. "Just open the damn door."

"I can't until the captain releases the security latch on the hatch."

Fifteen minutes later, Bob Pepper was sitting comfortably in his limousine as it drove off to Cape Neddick.

"What?" Clare spoke into her phone. "Bob, you are not needed here. Go home."

"Too late. You had the opportunity to keep me informed and failed Clarissa. I will be there in an hour."

"Bob?" The line had gone dead.

"Why is he coming here now?" Bill asked Clare, perturbed by this latest news.

"He is worried about all of us, and you know Bob Pepper. If he is not in the know, he gets upset. He wants to be kept informed at all times." Clare explained.

"More like he gets downright pissed off. We are not his publishing house, Clare." Bill replied.

"No, we are not." She agreed. "But he looks at all of us as his family. Especially your kids, Bill."

Vicky had been listening to their conversation from just inside the kitchen. She and Karen had gotten up early to start preparing breakfast and food for the upcoming day. "Grandpa Bob is coming here?" she asked.

"He'll be here in an hour, Vicky," Clare answered. "What smells so good? I'm starving."

"Bacon, sausage, hashbrowns, and white gravy are on the stove. Homemade biscuits are in the oven. I have blueberry pancake batter ready to go on the griddle, but I'm doing those and the eggs per order. This is kind of a walk-up and take-your-plate breakfast."

"Sounds yummy," Bill said. "I order first."

"Guests first," Vicky said sternly.

Clare shrugged. "Well, Doug and Logan should be here shortly. I couldn't sleep, so I came early, hoping I could help with something. You need help, Vicky?"

"I do need a few things from the grocery store."

"You have a list?" Clare asked, entering the kitchen. "I'll go. I need to swing by my house anyway."

Vicky handed her a piece of paper. "Please make sure the veggies are fresh. No canned stuff."

"You got it. Back soon."

As Clare headed toward the door, she passed Father Setzler and Father Dominic as they were coming down the grand staircase. "Sleep well?" She asked.

"Never better," Setzler replied. "I could use some coffee."

"Vicky is in the kitchen and can brew you some. Back soon!"

This would be the second time that Bob Pepper visited Shaw Manor. He had the opportunity in the past but just didn't seem to have found the time. Now that he had formally retired, it freed up enormous amounts of days on his calendar. What vacations he and Dottie had gone on seemed to be bucket list items, such as Northern Maine, New Hampshire, Vermont, and even Canada. Bob had fallen in love with the northeast and the few times they did travel had been limited by time. He was feeling guilty about not bringing his wife along on this trip but the uncertainty of what awaited warranted that she should remain at home.

This was the second time that Pepper had called on the Catholic church to intervene on behalf of the Penders. The priests had done little to nothing in the first instance, and he surmised that was why the demon still resided in their home. The one thing the old man was certain of was that he needed to be there this time. He wasn't sure why, but he could feel it in his gut.

"Grandpa!" Vicky ran to the man as he entered the front door, and she hugged him fiercely.

"Let me look at you, Vicky. I do believe you are taller." Bob Pepper said slyly.

"Liar. I haven't grown at all. Aerin has, though."

"Where is the lad?" He asked.

Aerin had been watching cartoons, but when he heard Vicky, he stood up and charged after her. He stopped and waited patiently for his sister to finish her hug before charging in to get one himself.

"There you are. I do believe you have grown."

"I missed you," Aerin said.

"Me too," Bob said, releasing the boy from his bear hug.

"Grandpa," Gaea said, walking up and giving him a brief hug and kiss. "I'm glad that you came. It's personal for you, isn't it? Being family and all."

"Yes, it is, and I thought you would understand of all people." He replied. "Let me get settled, and we can talk. Where is Bill and your mother?"

"Mom is taking a shower and Dad is up in the widow's watch. I can show you where it is, but the only way up to it is through their bedroom."

"I can wait."

Chrystal arrived and picked up his day bag. "Let me show you to your room, " she said, smiling.

"This house is full of angels, isn't it?" He replied with a wide grin. "Lead the way."

"Come back down soon. I'm cooking breakfast." Vicky said.

"I can smell it. I haven't had fresh biscuits and gravy in quite some time and yours are the best." Vicky blushed, turned, and ran back to the kitchen.

"My father was married before becoming a priest," Setzler said. "When my mother died at an early age, it broke his heart. I was a child and was sent to live with my grandmother. My dad chose to enter the priesthood, and along with his chosen path, he became an exorcist. As you know, I followed in his footsteps."

"I think we have an issue here and now to address," Bob said, leaning back in his chair.

"We do." Father Dominic said.

"It's afraid," Aerin said, stuffing another piece of bacon in his mouth.

"Afraid of what?" Bill asked.

"It's afraid of my brother, Dad. It's afraid of Aerin." Gaea answered.

The priests retired to the guest quarters above the garage to prepare for what was to come later that evening. Father Setzler felt it necessary to bring his superior up to speed on the rights of exorcism, as Father Dominic would be assisting even though he had not reviewed or performed the rites himself in the past. It was a straightforward process in theory, answering passages that Father Setzler would read, supporting the word of God to drive the demon from the possessed. In actuality, it was not so simple. The demon would undoubtedly resist and fight to retain what it believed was its property.

This situation was different as the foul beast was possessing the dead and trapping their souls, but it was also threatening the living. It had claimed it wanted Logan and Setzler had no intention to bend to the demon's demands. The priest had never been associated with so many gifted people in one location. He believed that Aerin was the one with the strongest abilities, and that was why the demon was afraid of the boy. From the onset, he knew that Aerin was needed at the manor for the exorcism but didn't fully know why. Now it was becoming clearer that strong mediums, along with the rites of exorcism delivered by the priests, would be needed to drive this demon out and save the souls at stake.

Father Setzler opened his satchel and handed a purple vestment along with a crucifix to Father Dominic. He pointed out the dozen vials of holy water that sat neatly within it. "We will read the prayers from the holy sacramental as well as the rights of exorcism. You will answer as the flock. There will come a time when we may have to attack the demon, and it may become dangerous. If I should falter you must not fail to finish. The demon must be cast out, or we will lose these souls and perhaps our own as well." Setzler explained.

"I understand the gravity of what we face, Father. Perhaps we should pray."

CHAPTER 25
An Ill Choice

Aerin did not seem concerned with what was happening around him, although he kept Logan nearby, watching TV or playing video games in his room. Doug was grateful that he was keeping an eye on his rambunctious young son, as he had the situation at hand to deal with. He also knew that his wife Clare was deathly afraid for Logan and wanted him out of the manor. Circumstances dictated otherwise.

Aerin could sense if there was a danger near his friend, and so far, he had no feeling of such. The manor remained calm and peaceful. Even the wind was nonexistent, allowing the snow to fall lightly on the estate grounds, although it was beginning to accumulate. "Winter has arrived," Doug said, prodding the fireplace with a poker.

"It's not even Thanksgiving yet," Cathy added, adjusting and playing with Gaea's hair. "You really need to get to the salon."

"Mom, please." The girl protested.

"It's getting cold as well," Bill said, looking out a window at a thermostat that was attached to the wall. "I'll turn up the furnace." Bill walked over to the kitchen to adjust the temperature.

"Maybe this will help," Vicky said, carrying a tray of mugs to the bar and setting it down on the countertop. "Warm eggnog, homemade, of course, minus the liquor."

"Kind of early for this, isn't it?" Doug asked. "Christmas is a long way away."

"Never too early for a holiday beverage." Bob Pepper commented and stood to examine the concoction presented. "Do you have any brandy, Bill?"

"I thought you gave up the drink," Bill said, smiling at his former boss.

"Scotch and yes, most of it. But having eggnog without a touch of brandy would be paramount to not putting whipped cream on your sundae." Bill smiled, opened the cabinet, and selected a bottle, placing it next to the tray. "Remy Martin," Bob said, examining the bottle. "Fine choice and not cheap."

"I've had it for years," Bill replied, smiling. "You gave it to me when I became a bestselling author."

"Now I recognize it. And you kept it all this time?"

"I don't drink brandy; however, if our resident chef recommends it for this delightful-looking eggnog, I think it is time to pop the cork. Vicky?"

"Brandy is perfect Dad. No rum and no bourbon." She replied, pulling another tray from the oven.

"How does she know about alcohol?" Pepper whispered.

"I heard that!" Vicky called from the kitchen. "It's a recipe thing. A small taste for cooking is allowed."

Bob rolled his eyes and went to get a cup. "Delicious as usual." He said, walking over and kissing Vicky on her cheek. "Who are those for?"

She placed the tray of warm cups next to the stove and began to ladle the eggnog into two of them. "Aerin and Logan."

"How thoughtful."

She sprinkled freshly ground nutmeg on top of the creamy liquid and wiped off a spilled drop from the tray with a dish towel. "I made enough for everyone to have as much as they want. If Father Dominic and Father Setzler want some, they can have it when they come back. I'm not going to bring it to them and bother what they are doing."

"Smart choice," Bob remarked and headed back toward the sitting area in front of the fireplace.

Vicky picked up the tray and headed up the back stairs. She was met at the top by Chrystal, who was washing a large window at the end of the hall. "Hey, Chris!" I made some eggnog to warm us up. Have Karen and Mrs. Douglas come down and have some."

"Yum! They are upstairs cleaning our quarters. I'll get them."

"Perfect!" Vicky replied and headed down the long hallway towards her brother's bedroom.

Aerin's room was located just after Vicky's. Further down was Gaea's and then her parent's master bedroom, separated by a large maid's closet. Directly across from that was the door that led up to the attic. The grand staircase was across from her parent's bedroom. In order to use the stairs, she would have to pass by that specific door where she had been attacked years ago and she was nervous every time she had to do so. Thus, Vicky chose to use the back servant stairs to go up to her room.

She knocked lightly on Aerin's door before opening it. The two boys were lying on the bed playing handheld video games that dated back to the late 1980s. "I brought you some eggnog that I made," Vicky said, placing the tray on the dresser. "Dad bought you a super gaming station, so why do you keep playing those old things?"

"Are you kidding?" Logan answered. "Tetris is so cool."

Aerin nodded and set his game down, taking a mug of the eggnog. "Yummy! Get yours, Logan."

The boy scrambled to pick up the mug, and taking a drink left a white foam mustache below his nose. Vicky laughed and headed out the door with the empty tray. "Keep this door locked, OK guys?" she asked.

"We will," Aerin answered.

Vicky closed the bedroom door and waited to hear the click of the lock setting in place. Satisfied, she turned to head back to the kitchen and stopped. Turning, she looked up the hall towards the attic door. "Get a grip, Vicky." She said quietly and walked slowly toward it. The door was held by two padlocks, and she could see that they were securely locked. A deadbolt had also been installed on the steel door, and the knob was keyed. Vicky sighed, then heard a muffled voice coming from the other side of the door.

"Victoria." It whispered.

"Daddy?"

"Victoria, come up here. You have been a very naughty girl."

The girl's eyes became wide, and she ran for the grand staircase charging down them screaming.

"I believe I know these rites well, Father Setzler. It has been some time since I read them, but they are coming back to me. I don't think I have them memorized, but reading them from the script should be no problem."

"That is good. This is no minor demon with which we are dealing. It is powerful and able to kill if allowed to." Dominic crossed himself and nodded.

"I don't think it knows how capable the gifted here are and will be taken aback once challenged. We need these people, Father."

"I agree, Father Setzler. I do, however, worry for the boy Logan."

"I am starting to think he may not be whom the demon wants. Remember who we are dealing with. It prefers males, and the accounts that are recorded tend toward adult men, although I don't think it is opposed to taking a child. That is our dilemma."

"I would think it will take whomever it can. The weakest."

"I concur, Father. Perhaps it is time to return to the manor." Setzler replied.

Doug met a hysterical Vicky in the great room at the bottom of the grand staircase. She collapsed into his arms, sobbing. "Vicky!" he exclaimed, embracing her. What is wrong?"

"It's my dad. He is in the attic! I heard him call to me through the door!"

"Baby, it's not him," Cathy said, running toward her daughter. "He died years ago."

"But Mom! I heard him!"

"I'll go check it out," Doug said. "The boys are up there, so I'll look in on them as well."

The girl nodded. "I'll go with you." Bill offered.

"No. I'm sure it will be fine. Stay here with Vicky. Hopefully, the priests will be back soon."

Doug headed up the stairs as Cathy comforted Vicky. As he approached the top of the second landing, everything was quiet. He could see that the door to Aerin's bedroom was closed. He walked to it, pausing at the closed attic door, noticing that it was securely padlocked shut. He put his ear to it but heard nothing. Continuing, he lightly knocked on the bedroom door.

"Come in." He heard his son Logan say.

"It's locked, dummy," Aerin replied. "I'll open it."

Doug was greeted by two boys looking at him curiously. "Are you two alright? I'm just checking to see if you need anything."

Aerin shook his head. "Vicky brought some eggnog, and we are just playing games."

"Nothing out of the ordinary?" Doug asked.

Both boys shook their heads. "No. Nothing." Aerin replied.

"Nope," Logan added.

"Good. I'll get you later for dinner and, um, keep the door locked." Doug closed the door and waited for a moment until he heard the lock click. Turning, he started to head toward the stairs and stopped in his tracks. The attic door stood wide open. As Doug approached it, he could see the two padlocks lying on the floor as if they had been opened by a key and dropped. The door was intact, unlike when it had been ripped off its hinges years before. He peered into the opening and up the narrow staircase into darkness. He reached in and flipped the light switch. The shattered light bulb had yet to be replaced.

"Hello?" He called out.

"I'm here," Clare answered from above.

"Honey? Why are you in the attic?"

"I need help, Doug. Please come."

He began to climb the stairs. Halfway to the top, the attic door slammed shut.

CHAPTER 26
Belphegor

Dominic and Setzler walked into the manor, followed by Clare toting two shopping bags and Lillian pulling up the rear. They were met by the sight of an upset Vicky, who was being cradled by Cathy. "What's going on?" Clare demanded, pushed by the priests, rushing to the kitchen and dropping the bags on the counter. "Where is Doug? Where is my son?"

"He went upstairs to check on the boys. Vicky thought she heard her father in the attic." Bill answered.

"It was him! I know it!" Vicky sobbed.

Father Dominic walked over and placed his hand on the girl's head. "It is not your father, child. The demon lies."

"But it sounded like him telling me to go to the attic. Like I was being punished all over again."

Cathy looked up at the priest. "He used to punish her by locking her in the attic."

"The demon knows this and uses the knowledge to deceive." Father Setzler said, opening his satchel. This will not be easy, but for dear Vicky, she is in no danger. I believe this."

"No, she is not," Aerin said, appearing from the servant stairs with Logan in tow.

"Logan!" Clare exclaimed and grasped her son in a hug.

"The attic door is open," Aerin said. "Why is it open?"

"What?" Gaea exclaimed, breaking off her conversation with Lillian.

"Yup. The locks are on the floor." He replied.

"This is not good." Bob Pepper spoke.

"No, it is not," Bill said, rushing to the washroom. "That's not possible." He said, returning with a small brass key dangling on a short piece of string. "The key to those locks was locked in a box above the washing machine."

"The demon is powerful." Father Setzler added.

"What about Doug?" Clare asked her son. "Did Dad check on you?"

"Yes." The boy replied. "He told us to keep the door locked and left. Didn't he come down?"

"I think we should head up to the attic, Father Dominic." Father Setzler stated. The priest nodded, and the two headed for the grand staircase. Setzler turned and addressed Gaea. "You and Bob will come as well as Lillian; however, please remain below unless called upon."

"I'm going up as well," Bill said flatly. "It's my daughter that could be going into harm's way."

The others nodded and chimed in, voicing that they wanted to go up as well. Father Setzler hushed them all. "The rest of you will stay down here unless needed and called upon. What is the adage? Too many cooks spoil the broth. No, you all will remain behind. This could take a great deal of time, and people will need sustenance, including myself and Father Dominic.

"I got it," Vicky said. "I have already been cooking."

Karen, Chrystal, and Mrs. Douglas had been standing quietly in the kitchen and quickly offered their services. "I've put the dog and the cat in my room for the time being," Karen said, fiddling with her apron.

"Smart thinking." Mrs. Douglas said, smiling. "No need to have pets underfoot during a crisis." The remainder of the group agreed to remain in the sitting room and look after the two boys.

"Very well," Setzler replied. "Let us go, Father."

The two exorcists climbed the grand staircase, followed by Gaea, Bob, Lillian, and Bill.

Dr. Jeffrey Tarpon drove south from Bath, Maine, with an uneasy feeling that he had not experienced in a long time. After a brief argument with his partner, Dr. Brambilla relented and watched as the car sped away from the dock.

Tarpon had had this feeling numerous times, dating back to his childhood. The feelings that he experienced were not dissimilar to a waking dream. He would have premonitions of things that had yet to pass. He had mostly ignored it, but at certain times, these visions had come to be factual. He had a waking dream while visiting the Penders and meeting Cathy for the first time. The vision was of someone falling from the balcony of the widow's watch. He had dismissed it. The most recent happening was at the ribbon cutting in Bath. A 'presence' in the manor was taunting him to go into the attic. He had mostly brushed that aside as well. However, it did cause him to begin a relentless search into online records and make numerous telephone calls. He knew that Cathy was a relative and believed that she was a first cousin. Now, he was having second thoughts, and if correct, they would have profound consequences for not only himself but for the entire Pender and Tarpon families.

He was a master at research, yet he had not turned up much pertaining to family records, either in Maine or in Canada. Records had been ill-kept, and a fire had erased a lot of them in Wells, Maine. He was able to determine that Cathy and his own mother may have been the same, as one record stated that they were both born in Montreal. He glanced at the document that rested on the passenger-side seat of the car. If he was correct, Cathy was not his cousin; she was his sister. Tarpon gripped the steering wheel of the Chevy and drove through the falling snow that brushed up and over the windshield, the wipers doing their best to clear the glass.

A foul stench emanated from the open door that led to the attic. Bill turned and nearly vomited on the floor as Gaea and Lillian covered their mouths and noses with their shirts.

"The smell of death," Dominic said.

"Do you not remember, Father? Leviticus chapter 14?"

"I do. But can it be leprosy?"

"It lies." The exorcist replied. "Let us proceed."

"Agreed."

Setzler glanced at Father Dominic, adjusted his purple vestment, and crossed himself, kissing his blessed crucifix. As he started up the stairs, he reached into the pocket of his robe, finding the aspergillum that held holy water. "Light the lantern, Father Dominic." And then he said softly, "Let Father Dominic and I confront the demon first. Stay on the stairwell until I call for you."

Climbing the stairs, Father Dominic placed his hand upon Setzler's shoulder; the odor from above becoming stronger. As the group made their way up, a low guttural growl echoed down from the attic stairwell. When the two priests arrived at the head of the stairs, Setzler was the first to see Doug slouched over in the chair just inside the range of the lantern light. His head was down, his chin resting on his chest, and his arms hung loosely by his sides. As they stepped onto the landing, Doug raised his head and glared at the priests with blood-red eyes.

"What do you want, priest?" He spat, saliva dripping from his bottom lip. "You have no power over me in this place."

Setzler placed a handkerchief over his mouth and looked at the creature that used to be a man before him. Sores covered its face, oozing green puss, and its lips were blistered. Its hair was matted, saturated with a thick ochre liquid that appeared to be drying mud mixed with blood. Bill turned and nearly vomited on the stairs from the stench, which would have covered Lillian as she and Bob were still standing behind him.

"You have no right to this man of God," Setzler said.

"He came to me, so he is mine. Another secondhand soul that I now own. The claim is mine to make." The demon growled.

"You are a liar, Belphegor." Father Dominic stated frankly.

"How do you know my name?" The demon demanded.

"You gave it up freely." Father Setzler answered reaching into his robe grasping the aspergillum as Bob charged up the stairs joining the two exorcists.

"You will not take him!" He said angrily toward the demon.

The demon sat back as it took in the new intrusion. "What is that doing here?"

"Enough, Belphegor," Setzler said and grasped his blessed holy cross. "Father Dominic, the vestments."

Dominic opened his Bible as the exorcist walked forward, placing his left hand on Doug's forehead while holding the end of his stole on the demon's neck. "Ecce crucem Domini." The exorcist Setzler said, and the demon growled, lunging forward. Bob Pepper came off his feet and flew to the far wall hitting it and collapsing into unconsciousness.

"Another secondhand soul that will belong to me." Belphegor laughed, sitting back on the chair. "And a powerful one."

The exorcist uncapped the vial of holy water and splashed it over the demon, causing it to scream. The two priests continued to recite the rights of exorcism. Bill charged up the stairs and rendered aid to Bob's side. Gaea turned to Lillian and spoke softly. "Go and bring Aerin. Only my brother. Do not tell Clare or my mom anything about Doug. OK?" Lillian nodded and headed back down the stairs.

"You cannot hide, Belphegor. You possess the living and will be cast out!" Setzler shouted.

In the great room, Aerin looked up toward the ceiling and stood up. "Stay here. They need me."

"It's too dangerous!" His mother declared, looking at her son.

Aerin's eyes turned from brown to blue and back to brown, and he smiled. "Trust me, Mother. Lillian, you stay as well."

Tarpon became increasingly worried as he approached the turnoff that led to Perkins Cove and the road that would take him to Cape Neddick. The snowfall had increased and was making it difficult to drive. He had never driven these roads before, yet he had memories and knew that parts of the road could be dangerous. How he knew, he had no clue, yet he had the fervent desire to get to Shaw Manor. Turning a corner, he nearly lost control as a truck came at him from the opposite direction, blowing its horn and startling him. Cursing under his breath, he gripped the steering wheel and pressed on.

Aerin looked up as he climbed the grand staircase alone. Upon reaching the landing, the boy could hear the priests as they battled with the demon. As he turned the corner and approached the open attic door, he heard a yell and a dull thud followed by Gaea screaming. Stepping into the doorway he looked up the staircase. Aerin could see his sister standing at the head of the stairs with her hands covering her mouth, crying. One of the priests was lying on the stairs, his head toward where he stood. Blood seeped from a gash on the man's forehead. He could see no one else but could hear the other priest fighting with the demon.

"In the name of God, I cast you out!"

The demon growled. "Another secondhand soul for me." It laughed and spoke again. "Dominic will make a nice addition, and you have no power here, Setzler. Leave before I decide to take yours as well."

Aerin had heard enough and quickly climbed the stairs stepping over the limp body of Father Dominic. He looked at his sister and smiled. Gaea looked back into her brother's blue eyes, which seemed to glow with an aura. In an instant, they turned back to deep brown. "Don't worry." He said softly and turned to face the demon.

The exorcist had fallen to one knee holding up the crucifix. He dropped the empty vial of holy water onto the floor and wept. Aerin placed his hand on the priest's shoulder. "Let me." He said softly. Father Setzler nodded and retreated, joining Gaea.

"Ah, the child has arrived," Belphegor said gruffly. "You are the one I desire, so I am glad you have come to me."

"I am not here to join you, demon, but to banish you."

"Ha! You are nothing more than a child—a gifted one, but still a child. You will make a nice addition to my collection, " the demon said, waving its hand toward the far end of the attic, where the apparitions of Tracy, Rebecca, and Father Dominic stood before the window, all three glowing in a red aura.

 Gaea ran to join her father as Father Setzler collapsed against the stairwell wall. "Dad! Is Grandpa okay?" She asked, crouching by his side.

"I think so. A bump on the head knocked him out."

"I'm afraid!" Gaea sobbed.

"Look." Her father said.

Aerin had approached the demon and stood no more than a few feet from the beast. It resembled Doug, but the likeness was no more than that of a corpse. Cuts, bruises, and sores seeped a disgusting greenish goo that covered his body and reeked of vile odor that permeated the attic. The demon lunged but was forced back into the chair on which it sat by something it could not comprehend.

"How?" The demon croaked. "You should be dead."

Aerin's eyes changed from brown to pure blue and began to emanate a white aura that grew, engulfing the boy's body. "I am here to banish you."

"It's not possible."

As Bill, Gaea, and Father Setzler looked on, Aerin grew and transformed before their eyes, becoming an eight-foot-tall being with silver hair that draped to its waist, its head nearly touching the manor's rafters.

"Michael! You have no right to be here!" Belphegor growled angrily.

"I have every right. Demon, you have none."

Father Setzler sat wide-eyed as he looked on. "Can it be?" He whispered to himself.

The demon pushed back, trying to slide the chair away. It then tried to get up but was forced back.

"You will not escape, Belphegor. All ends here."

"Michael, the Archangel of God, protector of all humanity." The exorcist said aloud.

"What?" Gaea asked from a few feet away.

"He is the most powerful of all of God's angels," Setzler replied.

"Michael, you cannot do this to me." Belphegor pleaded.

Wings appeared on the angel's back and stretched from one side of the attic to the other. Michael withdrew his sword and held it in front of his armor, its aura glowing blue. "It is not mine to command, I simply follow and obey as you should have."

"Please, my brother."

"You are not my brother, Belphegor." The arch angel stated and drove the sword through Doug's chest.

The demon screamed, and the angel withdrew the blade. Doug collapsed in the chair. Michael turned and addressed Father Setzler. "It is over. You performed well, and all who remain are safe. The rest will be allowed to enter unto the grace of God." The priest could not utter a word and simply nodded.

"Daddy?" Gaea asked, clutching her father.

"Wait," he whispered.

Gaea watched as the archangel grasped the sword against its breast plate, closed his eyes, and, looking up, turned the aura into a bright, white, blinding light. Upon adjusting back to the dimness of the lantern light, Gaea could see her brother standing where Michael once stood, and she rushed to his side. She hugged him fiercely and looked into his deep brown eyes. "What happened?" he asked.

"I'm not sure." She replied. "Let's go downstairs."

Bob had recovered and, other than being groggy, was able to have Bill help him down the stairs. Setzler stood and checked on Doug, who, although groggy as well, was recovering. Most of the sores and blemishes had vanished from his skin, while some bruises remained. "Can you walk, my friend?" the priest asked.

"Give me a few minutes," Doug replied.

Setzler nodded and turned to the far end of the attic, where the apparitions of Dominic, Tracy, and Rebecca stood aglow in a blue light. All had smiles on their faces. The exorcist approached the trio and stood before Father Dominic. "It is time to go, " he said simply, and the apparition vanished. Tracy was next as Setzler stood before her. You as well, my dear. Your purgatory is done here. Go rest." She nodded and vanished.

"As for you, my child, your time is not yet at hand. Your mother has been searching for you for an exceptionally long time, and she waits for you in the courtyard below. Go to her." Rebecca smiled and nodded, turned, and passed through the attic window. Setzler crossed himself and returned to Doug. "Come, my friend, loved ones await you."

CHAPTER 27
Shaw Manor

Bill appeared at the bottom of the grand staircase, supporting Bob Pepper with his arm around the older man's waist. As the two made their way into the great room, Lillian ran to help. "What happened?" She asked.

"A lot, but it's over."

"Where is Aerin?" Cathy demanded, confronting her husband.

"He is fine as well and should be down in a moment. If it wasn't for him, I think we might all be dead."

"And Gaea?"

"I'm here, Mom, " the girl said, leading her brother off the stairs and toward the others.

"Thank God," Cathy exclaimed and ran toward her children grasping them both in a hug.

Vicky joined them, sobbing. "I was so worried."

Logan grasped his mother's hand and looked up at her. "Mom?"

"I know, honey." She said nervously. "And Doug?"

"I'm not sure," Bill replied. "He was possessed by the demon."

"What?" Clare asked, astonished.

Father Setzler came down the stairs with Doug in tow and interrupted. "It seems that Belphegor was using your husband to get at Aerin, and it would have worked except for divine intervention."

"Where is Father Dominic?" Cathy asked.

"Ah, perhaps the authorities should be called. Father Dominic is no longer with us." Hearing this, Mrs. Douglas reached for the kitchen phone.

"What about Jack?" Gaea asked.

"He was never here." Father Setzler answered. "It was a ruse by the demon."

Clare ran to her husband's side and stroked his face. "Look at you; you're all bruised. Are you okay? What happened?"

Doug smiled weakly and plopped onto the sofa near the fireplace. "I don't remember much. I would like a scotch. I hurt all over, especially the middle of my chest."

"I'll get it," Vicky said and ran to the bar.

Karen and Chrystal shuffled nervously in the kitchen listening intently to the tale being told.

"What do you mean by divine intervention?" Lillian asked.

The priest sat on a chair near the fireplace and smiled weakly. "It seems that our Aerin was touched by the hand of a very powerful servant of God."

The winter storm was still dropping vast amounts of snow as Tarpon pulled into the drive that led up to Shaw Manor. He drove carefully, and as he neared the top of the hill, he could see red and blue lights circling and flashing ahead. Pulling into the drive, he was met with the sight of two police cars, a ladder truck, and an ambulance. For a moment, he thought he could see a woman in a long dress holding the hand of a young girl running across the snow-covered estate lawn and disappearing into the blinding storm. He shook his head. "Dammit." He muttered and pulled up and parked next to one of the police cars. Climbing out, he was immediately met by an officer who challenged him.

"Sir. This is an ongoing crime scene. What is your business here?" The officer asked.

"I'm Catherine Pender's brother," Tarpon responded. "Where is she?"

"Come with me." She said and headed for the front door of the manor.

Police and firefighters had invaded the manor and were busy combing the upstairs. Doug downed his second scotch and asked for another. Bob Pepper had asked for one also. A paramedic was tending to Doug's bruises and the few small cuts that were on his face when Jeffrey Tarpon came into the room.

"Ma'am?" The officer said to Cathy. "This gentleman claims to be your brother."

Cathy's mouth fell agape. "Well, yes. Yes, he is. Thank you for coming, Jeffrey." She walked and hugged the scientist and feigned a kiss on his cheek. "What?" She whispered.

"I believe this to be true," Tarpon said, handing her the manilla envelope. "Let me explain later. It seems that there is an issue to be dealt with at the moment."

Cathy nodded. "Vicky?"

"Yes, Mom?"

"Uncle Jeff is here. How about an eggnog or something?"

Bill was as confused as Vicky but remained silent.

"Dad?' Gaea asked quietly. "Uncle Jeff?"

Bill shrugged.

Everyone was interrupted by the heavy boots of the firefighters on the grand staircase as they made their way down to the great room, followed by two uniformed police officers and a plain-clothed detective. The detective approached the family and shook his head. "There is nothing up in the attic." He said, tucking a notepad into his pocket. "I'm not sure what you all are trying to pull here. The only things up there are a few boxes, a mannequin, and an old chair."

Bill looked at the priest and then his wife.

"Detective, I think I might have the answer," Doug said, placing his glass of scotch on the table. "I was up there, well, looking for the cat. I slipped on the steps and fell, hitting my head. I thought I saw a body on the stairs, but I was dizzy."

The paramedic spoke up. "That is very plausible. Mike, he seems to have a concussion."

"Hmm. Maybe he needs to go to the hospital, Pete. Concussions are nothing to play with." The detective offered.

"Only if he agrees to go." The paramedic replied and turned his attention back to Doug. "Sir?"

"No, I'm fine," Dough said, smiling. "What would they do? Tell me to lay in bed and do nothing for a week or so?"

"Probably." The paramedic answered. "But I am just an EMT and not a doctor. Do you want to go?"

"No," Doug said flatly.

"Nothing I can do, Mike. He is coherent and can refuse treatment and transport."

"In that case, let's wrap it up. Julia, can you stay and draft the report?" The detective asked a young officer.

The young policewoman nodded. "There's not much to log here."

"Nevertheless, you know the protocol."

She nodded, turned, and left.

An hour later, after a cup of Vicky's warm eggnog, both the police and the firemen had left. All but Officer Julia, who sat in her patrol car on the driveway drafting the report.

Father Setzler tried to explain how an archangel could possess the body of a child to battle an evil demon but there was no explanation to give. There was no precedent in the history of the Catholic Church or any religion of the earth, and he had no knowledge of such in the archives of the Vatican. The disappearance of Dominic's body was also a mystery. Setzler was dumbfounded but elated and uplifted by what he had witnessed. His faith had been shored up by the appearance of Michael the archangel, the highest of the angels that served God's will.

"It's time for me to leave." Father Setzler said, standing and heading for the door. He placed his fedora on his head as Bill opened the door for him. "I must report to my superiors. There is much to explain."

"Thank you, Father," Bill said, accompanying the priest to the door.

"Do not thank me. I would have failed if it were not for Aerin and Archangel Michael. I will not fail the next time I face such a demon."

"I believe you," Bill said and closed the door behind the exorcist.

"Now, what nonsense did you use to get into my house?" Cathy demanded, confronting Jeffrey.

"Catherine, I believe it is true. Read the data in the packet, and I think you will agree. Our mother and father are the same."

Cathy slumped onto the couch and tore into the envelope, and removing the paperwork, she started to read. Moments later, she looked up at Tarpon in disbelief.

Julia was finishing her report by the glow of her center console computer. The snow still fell heavily, and her cruiser's windshield wipers struggled to keep up with clearing it off the glass. She was distracted by the security light in the garage turning on and looked up. She thought she saw a woman crossing in front of it, holding a young girl's hand. "What the?" She muttered and climbed out of her car. The snow blinded her, and she could not see anyone. Climbing back in, she shook her head, turned off the computer, and started the car. She drove slowly down the driveway, anxious to get home.

The snow-covered woods sparkled in the dim moonlight as Lily and Rebecca made their way down the long pathway. The old path led along the estate wall that separated the woods from the ocean. Rebecca giggled and skipped, although her feet did not touch the earth as they both glided over the icy ground. Her mother looked down at her daughter, picked her up, and the two danced together, twirling in the falling snow. Arriving at the iron gates, they passed through the bars entering the cemetery, vanishing into the wintery darkness of the night.

A Few Off the Old Royal:

The Widow's Watch: A Haunting on Cape Neddick (1 of 3)

The Widow's Watch: Dreamer's Hideaway (2 of 3)

The Widow's Watch: Shaw Manor (3 of 3)

Tales of the Little Lagoon: Kiwa's Story

The Dream Catcher

Spirits and Tales

One with Paper In:

Gaea & The Night Witch
(*A Continuation of the Widow's Watch Series (Book 1)*)

9 798999 862323